MATES AT WAR

Ronald Botham

ARTHUR H. STOCKWELL LTD
Torrs Park   Ilfracombe   Devon
Established 1898
www.ahstockwell.co.uk

*British Library Cataloguing-in-Publication Data.
A catalogue record for this book is available
from the British Library.*

*This is an entirely fictional story,
and no conscious attempt has been made
to accurately record or recreate
any real-life events.*

ISBN 978-0-7223-4005-9
*Printed in Great Britain by
Arthur H. Stockwell Ltd
Torrs Park   Ilfracombe
Devon*

CONTENTS

Prelude

It was 7.30 a.m., November 1941. Tom Weston woke up and looked out of the window over the bleak and cold inlet near Harwich, where the 14th Flotilla motor torpedo boats were anchored. Sub Lieutenant Tom Weston of the Royal Navy, twenty years of age, already over fifty sorties completed, looked out at the bleak scene and wondered what Saturday 20 November would bring. He had been through Dunkirk and numerous sorties against the Germans already. He was the holder of the Distinguished Service Cross and he felt forty years old, not twenty.

He had been stationed here for four months now. Tom looked across the room at the other occupant, Sub Lieutenant Charlie Higson; they were best mates and the same age and had joined up together in 1937. They trained together and volunteered for the Small Boats section in October 1938.

Tom was five foot eleven inches tall, fourteen stone with tousled blonde hair and striking blue eyes. He played rugby and he was definitely a ladies' man. Charlie was five foot nine inches, dark-haired, with a beard which made him look older than his years, but he always seemed to get the girls. Charlie commanded Motor Torpedo Boat 324, whilst Tom had 326. There was a flotilla of six boats, all seventy foot long with a nineteen-foot beam, with room to live on board if need be. Built in the US, each had two Vosper-type Packard engines of 1250 b.h.p., giving a top speed of over 40 knots. Two torpedo tubes, twin Browning machine guns on either side of the bridge, a 20-millimetre cannon forward, a Bofors gun and a twin 20-metre cannon on the stern gave plenty of firepower.

Tom's crew consisted of Sub Lieutenant Harry Barnes, aged twenty-three years, as his number one; Petty Officer 'Yorkie'

Cowling, engineer; Leading Seaman Reg Thomas, wireless operator; Sub Lieutenant John Green, DSC, navigator; Chief Petty Officer Dave Hill, coxswain; Able Seaman Bob Crowe and Able Seaman Stan Grey on the forward cannon; Able Seaman Jimmy Townsend and Able Seaman Walter Brown on the twin Brownings; Able Seaman Les Wright and Able Seaman Todd Soames on the Bofors gun; Leading Seaman Jock McLeish on the stern cannon; and Petty Officer George Davies and Petty Officer Bill Roe on torpedoes.

This is a story of this close-knit crew, and how they fought together through the early days of the Second World War.

CHAPTER 1

Briefing

The commanding officer, Lieutenant Commander James Dolin had called a briefing at 1400 hours that day, and as all the crews piled into the ops room they wondered what this one was for. On the platform were second in command, Lieutenant Robson, DSC; civilian weatherman, Arthur Rollings; and 1st Officer Natalie James (WRNS). They could all see the long covered map on the wall.

"Looks like something big," Tom muttered to Charlie, who was busy looking at 1st Officer Natalie James's legs. Tom nudged him. "I know what you are thinking," he said, "but I think the CO's got first call."

"No harm in thinking!" said Charlie.

At that moment the CO stepped on to the platform. The second in command yelled "Attention!" and they all stood straight as he walked in. An impressive man, Lieutenant Commander Dolin was six foot one inch, quite broad and handsome.

"OK, relax. You can smoke if you want to."

He had been in the navy since he was a boy; now he was twenty-nine years old, with a Distinguished Service Order, and, as everyone in the room would tell you, he was a terrific CO. He was brave but not reckless, and he always insisted no one would be left behind after an operation unless recovery was impossible. Every man in the flotilla was prepared to give his life for this man. Dolin was married to Jenny, and they had two children, a boy and a girl, whom he idolised; and, whatever the others thought, he would not look at another woman.

He began the briefing:

"This is a big one – a German convoy of twelve ships and a large escort. Intelligence informs us it consists of two tankers, an ammunition ship, five cargo vessels, three troop carriers, an auxiliary boat and an escort of boats including destroyers."

The muttering from the crowd said it all.

"Blimey!" Todd exclaimed. "That's not big; it's bloody enormous!"

"All right," said the CO, "settle down. Our flotilla, along with the 14th, 10th and 18th Flotillas, will also be in on this one. So that's a total of twelve motor torpedo boats and four motor gun boats."

Dolin asked for the map to be displayed, at which there was a gasp from the company. He strolled over, picked up a billiard cue and turned to the audience. There was a hush.

"Now," he said, pointing to the Hook of Holland, "on the 23rd of November, this convoy will sail from Rotterdam. As you can imagine, it will cover a large area of sea. Our job is to inflict as much damage as possible. Time of sailing, we have been informed, is 2200 hours on that date. We estimate the speed of the convoy will be 12 to 15 knots; the plan of attack is to select an area to strike at 0030 hours – hit hard and fast. The MTBs of the 10th Flotilla will strike first, and then the MGBs will follow in on the escorts. We will follow in on the other side so as to divide their defence; we will hit hard and with all the firepower we have, and if we can hit the ammunition ship, that should cause panic. That's the plan, now for the position of your flotillas. Take note. Pick your targets, strike and get out."

The briefing went on for another hour. Call signs and positions were allocated; notes on the weather reports were taken. The CO closed the meeting and wished everyone good luck and a safe return. Then he asked Tom to stay behind.

Charlie said, "It looks like you are going to get a special job."

"Why me?" said Tom. "We are no better than the rest of the crews."

"You'll soon know," said Charlie. "Anyway, let me know what happens, mate."

"I will," said Tom.

With that, Charlie left and Tom called his crew together.

"Please sit down," said the CO. "Tom, you and your crew are the most experienced on this op so we've got a special job for you; you will leave one hour before the rest of us. It won't be easy, but we want you to follow the convoy and supply us with up-to-date info. All frequencies and any positions are on this file. Read and digest it before you sail. If we can pull this off, it will cause panic in Jerry HQ. That's all I want to say. No one else needs to know you are going early – say nothing to anyone."

With that, the CO left and the lads gathered round to hear what Tom had to say.

"I know I can rely on you. I couldn't wish for a better crew. We've got all day tomorrow to prepare, so let's make sure the boat is in primo condition. Anything you want, let me know and I will arrange it. You all know what to do, so I suggest you all take it easy for the rest of the day; we all have an early start tomorrow. Any questions?"

"Do we get double time for this?" asked Todd.

This brought an outburst of laughter from the lads.

"No! You will probably get your pay docked for your cheek," was the reply.

This was followed by the usual banter as the boys left the ops room. Tom proceeded to meet Charlie, who was waiting in another room.

"Well, what happened? Have they made you an admiral?"

"No," said Tom, laughing. "I will tell you this, though – but it goes no further."

"OK," replied Charlie, "go on."

"We are leaving an hour before the rest of you to shadow the Jerries and pass on info."

"Blimey!" said Charlie. "That could be dodgy, but they've picked the right guy in you to do it."

"Thanks," said Tom. "Let's go out for a meal tonight. How about it?"

"Suits me," said Charlie. "Are we going to look for some female company whilst we're at it?"

"Why not?" Tom said. "We'll try that place we went to a while back."

"Well, let's get tarted up and go. Hey! I want first chance this time – you always get first chance," answered Tom.

"I know that, but I always finish up with the other bird. Well, never mind, they are usually all dishy anyway. Come on, then – let's get changed." Charlie stopped suddenly. "Hey, do we have enough dosh for a good night out and girls?"

"We'll have to have, so get changed and hurry up about it."

As Tom started to get ready, he suddenly thought, 'Oh, God, this could be the last time we will be doing this.' This would be no ordinary job, and he'd done enough ops to know that. As he stepped into the shower, he thought, 'Ah, well, let's just enjoy ourselves.' Thirty minutes later he looked in the mirror and thought, 'OK, I've done my best. Let's go.'

Charlie looked across the room and said, "Come on, Tom – I feel lucky tonight. Let's go."

The next morning Tom and his crew were up early. After breakfast they went to the boat to make sure everything would be in tip-top condition for the op.

"Check all the guns and torpedoes," said Tom. "You know what to do, lads."

They had a tea break at about 1100 hours and then worked through till 1400 hours, after which Tom got them all together.

"Everything in top shape?" he asked.

"Couldn't be better," said the chief.

"OK," said Tom. "Well, get cleaned up and have some rest and something to eat."

Charlie came over as the men were leaving. "Everything OK?" he asked Tom.

"I think so now," he said. "Hey, how did you get on with that bird last night?"

"OK," replied Tom, but not as well as I expected to."

"I thought she was a cert. Mine was great."

"Well, one up to you," said Tom. "Will you see her again?"

"No such luck!" Charlie replied. "She's off up north to work."

"That's life!" Tom replied. "OK, let's go get some rest and eat; it looks like an early night."

"Yeah," said Charlie, "a couple in the mess, then early to bed."

"After you," said Tom.

The CO was sitting at his desk. First Officer James knocked on the door.

"Come in. Hello, Natalie. What is it?"

"A phone call from your wife, sir."

"Oh, right," he replied. "I'll take it through here."

Natalie left the room. She adored her CO, but she knew there was no chance for her there. She had met his wife and children; Helen was a very striking woman and the children were lovely. She knew this was a tricky and dangerous mission that they were about to undertake, and she knew he wouldn't tell his wife. She realized how difficult it must be for Helen when he went off on missions and she never knew what dangers he was facing.

The CO finished his call and rang for Natalie to come through into the office.

"Sit down, Natalie; I've something I want to say to you. As you know, I never tell Helen about the ops, including this one. I also know how you feel about me. I don't have to tell you how much I appreciate all you do for me, and you know how fond of you I am."

"I know that, sir, but I'm not jealous of Helen – you know that – and I adore your children."

"Yes," said the CO, "that's why if anything happens to me, I want you to be the one to tell my wife. She thinks you are a very special lady, and I know she would rather hear it from you than some damned telegram. Anyway, now I've got that out of the way, I would like you to have dinner with me when all this is over. I've told Helen and she says you deserve that much. She admires your loyalty and, you know, Helen, she doesn't have a bad thought for anyone. Well, I'm glad we've had this chat. Now I'm off to see that the crew and boats are all OK. They are a great bunch, and I'm very proud of them. While I'm doing that, will you make sure all the papers are in order? I want you to take them to the Commodore personally."

"Oh, OK," she said quietly.

Secretly, she didn't like Commodore Harris. He was good at his job, but he had wandering hands and lecherous roving eyes. He had tried several times to get her to go out with him –

unsuccessfully, of course – but he was a determined man and very intimidating at times. He worried her, but she hadn't mentioned it to anyone as she didn't want to find herself posted away. She had her duty to do, and she would do it.

CHAPTER II

The Attack

It was 2100 hours as 326 left its berth. It was dark and a drizzle was beginning to fall.

"Take her out easy," said Tom. He was checking his instructions down in the chart room below the bridge with John Green.

"It's going to be a murky night," said John.

"It sure is," replied Tom.

"We will have to be especially on the lookout tonight, so we will make for the first position and take it from there. It should take about two hours to make it if the sea is calm."

Gunners Les Wright and Todd Soames were sitting by the ammo locker.

"I wonder if we will find the convoy," said Todd.

"Course we bleedin' will," replied Les. "It will take up half the bloody ocean – I shouldn't think we could miss it."

"The engines sound sweet tonight," said Reg.

"Aye, they do that," replied Yorkie. "Let's hope they stay that way."

"Well, they should do after all the work we have done on them," Reg shouted. "These Packards are bloody reliable."

The rest of the crew were busy checking their own equipment.

"I hope we can get some test-firing in," said Jimmy Townsend.

"It would be unusual if you don't," said Dave Hill; he was concentrating on the wheel.

At that Harry arrived on the bridge.

"I've been round the boat – we are in good shape, sir," he

said to Tom. "We can have a quick test-firing and everything will be OK, chief."

The number one arrived on the bridge.

"Everything OK?" Tom asked.

"A1," said Harry.

"Good. In thirty minutes we will have a quick test-firing, and then we'll have a brew. What speed are we doing?" he asked.

"Fifteen knots, sir; we're on course for 0700. That should give us plenty of time to get in position. I'll go get a cuppa organised. The brew should warm us up," Harry said. "I thought it should get plenty bloody warm enough when we find that bloody convoy."

"It certainly will," replied Tom. "It's the biggest one we have ever tackled. I hope the Jerries think they are too big to be attacked."

"I don't think they are that stupid," Dave replied.

"Me neither," Tom answered, "but they will get a hell of a shock when our lot turn up. Anyway, it's too to late to worry about that now. Let's just get our part right."

The brew came round and the crew devoured a few corned-beef sandwiches, after which a test-firing was completed.

"Well," said Tom, "all we've got to do now is find the bloody convoy."

"I shouldn't think we will be able to miss it," said Harry. "We've just got to make sure they don't spot us first."

One hour later, 326 departed. The rest of the groups began to depart from the ports to make for the rendezvous. The timing had to be spot-on, they all knew that.

Lieutenant Commander Dolin, leading 14th Flotilla, turned to his number one, Bill Kirkbride, and said, "Well, that's the first part done. If Weston does his part right, it should be quite a party."

"Well, if there's one person we can rely on, it's Tom Weston. He is the right man to do it. I've every confidence in him, haven't you?"

"I wouldn't have asked him if I hadn't," replied the Commander. "If this comes off, I think he'll get his second ring – and he will have earned it."

"If this comes off," said Kirkbride, "we'll all have earned it, I should think."

"Let's hope it does. If we can wreck that bloody convoy, it'll give Jerry a headache and plenty to think about."

"It will that, but like you said, sir, overall we aren't doing very well in this war. You can only try and win your own battles, and I think we are going a long way to doing that."

"We are," said the Commander, "and we've got to keep on doing that." Checking his watch, he said, "Tom should be in position in about thirty minutes. Tell the wireless operator to keep a sharp ear open; he will only send a very short signal. Once we've received it we'll get in position for the main attack. The signal will be red over green for the show to begin."

Meanwhile in the ops room, back at base, Natalie was sitting in the gallery overlooking the plot. On the plot was 1st Officer Marion Baines and four Wren plotters. Lieutenant Stuart Watson was in charge of plot and signals. They were standing together talking. Marion and Stuart had been together for about six months now. Stuart was married to a Northumberland girl, Mary, who was at this moment in Scapa Flow.

Stuart said, "I really enjoyed last night, darling. Did you?"

"I did," replied Marion, "but don't let's forget you are married. We both agreed that this is just a fling and nothing more than that."

Stuart said, "I know, but sometimes I feel it's more than just a fling."

Marion looked at him and replied, "No, love. If it starts to get serious, we both agreed to end it."

Natalie was watching them; she knew what was going on as Marion had told her. She felt a little jealous. She thought, 'I wish the Commander felt the same way.' But she knew that would never happen. Marion had said she could fix her up with Stuart's friend, Alan, but Natalie had said no. She just wasn't ready for that at the moment.

The door opened, and who should walk in but Commodore Harris.

'Oh, hell!' she thought. 'I'm not having him bothering me tonight.'

He hadn't spotted her, so she made a hasty retreat through the side door.

Marion saw her go. She said to Stuart, "Excuse me, love, you'd better go and greet the Commodore. I have to go to the ladies' room."

Outside she saw Natalie coming down the stairs. "Hi, love," she said. "You escaping?"

"Oh, yes," said Natalie. "I can't stand that man near me."

"You're not on your own. Anyway, he will be too occupied to bother you while the op's on. If he asks, I'll tell him you've gone on a forty-eight-hour pass. I know he's our superior officer, but he's a bloody nuisance. His wife is arriving tomorrow; if I can get close to her, I might just have to have a casual word in her ear. She knows what he is like."

"Oh, Marion, I wish you would," said Natalie. "I'd love to be there when you do it, but it's best if I keep out of the way. Besides, we'll all be too busy with the boats returning."

"You leave it to me, love," said Marion. "I'll scuttle his plans."

Natalie knew she wasn't kidding; she was a lot older, and wise in the ways of dealing with men.

On 324 Charlie was on the bridge waiting for the signal for the balloon to go up.

'I hope Tom's OK,' he thought. 'We'll have to have a bloody good party after this lot is over – God willing!'

He turned to his number one, Alan Kelly. "Keep her steady," he said. "It won't be long before that signal comes through. Can you nip round the boat and make sure the lads are ready?"

"Right, sir," said Alan.

Alan was only nineteen years old and Charlie thought of him as the baby of the ship; Charlie knew he was feeling apprehensive, but he also knew he wasn't the only one. Keeping busy was the best thing he knew of to keep your mind off what was about to happen.

Off Alan went.

"Watch it there, young Alan," said Chief Petty Officer Don Taylor. "You OK?"

"Yes, thanks, Chief. The skipper just asked me to nip round and check on the lads."

"Just keep yourselves busy, and you'll all be fine," said Taylor.

This was Alan's first action with 326; he had seen action before, but not like this and he was determined not to let anyone down.

As he went, the Chief turned to his companion and said, "That lad will make a good officer one day."

"Aye," relied his mate. "That's if he survives this lot," he added.

"Why are you so bloody miserable?" said the Chief.

"Well, you know it's being so happy that keeps me going," said his mate.

With that, they both laughed. The Chief knew his mate was one of the bravest guys going.

"Well, here goes!" said Tom. They had sighted the convoy five minutes earlier, and they had noted the position, speed and time. "We'll let them get past and then get that signal off. I'm off to the chart room now, so keep her steady and keep your eyes peeled. As soon as they've passed, let me know."

It was pitch black and clouded over – not a star to be seen – in fact, ideal for what they needed to do.

Tom entered the chart room.

"Well, John, we've sighted them, so get ready to send that signal fast because all hell's about to break loose. Stay at the radio in case anything comes back, and let me know straight away. I'm off to the bridge," said Tom.

"OK, sir. I'll take her now."

"This is it, so tell the lads it's on; stand by to attack as soon as they see the signal red over green. We will take the last vessel in line and try to cause confusion at the rear. Watch out for our boats coming through, especially 14th Flotilla. They're gonna be coming in fast."

The flares red over green burst above the convoy; at the same time, several star shells burst, lighting up the scene.

Tom shouted, "NOW! Get that last bloody ship."

He pushed open the throttles and 326 leapt forward. The twin Browning opened up along with the forward cannon. Tom saw the tracers snaking out, striking the cargo vessel; they were doing 30 knots as both torpedoes were fired. Tom turned the wheel to port, and as they ran along the convoy the Bofors and stern cannon opened up. Tom could see they were hitting ship after ship.

Suddenly there was a hell of a bang. The sky lit up as the ammunition ship went up. It must have taken other boats with it, as fires were going up all over the convoy. They had taken it completely by surprise. As Tom steered the boat away, a tracer shot across and over the boat, but luckily there were no hits.

He yelled, "Keep your eyes open for the escort."

At that moment an E-boat cut across them and fired, the green and white tracers finding their mark. Tom heard a bang.

Harry shouted, "They've hit the Bofors."

"Get down there and see what the damage is," shouted Tom.

He felt a pain in his side and shouted to get any casualties below. There were explosions and firing going on all around now.

"Time to get out!" he yelled, and with that he opened the throttles further and the boat sped away.

They had been hit several times and they had wounded. Again he felt the pain in his side, but he ignored it. He saw a boat on fire as they sped away.

"Look," said the coxswain, who was back on the bridge, "one of ours is in trouble."

"I see him," yelled Tom. "We'll go over to see if there is anything we can do."

They were about a mile away from the convoy by now. As they made their way towards the stricken boat he could see the convoy had been badly mauled. He slowed down and came alongside the stranded boat.

"Keep your eyes peeled for Jerry," he shouted.

As they came alongside, the coxswain and his number one were helping survivors into their boat. He knew he hadn't much time, but he was determined not to leave anyone on that boat.

The coxswain shouted, "I think we have got them all. I think she is gonna blow."

As they pulled away the boat blew up.

'God, I hope we got them all off,' thought Tom.

Orange and white flares shot up into the sky, signalling the withdrawal. Tom pushed open the throttles again and the boat leapt forward. Other boats were now joining them. He looked at his watch – the whole attack had only lasted twenty minutes. As he looked back, he could see explosions and fires all over the sea.

"Take over," he shouted. "I'll see what we've got."

The coxswain grabbed the wheel, but as he did Tom went over on his side.

"Skipper's been hit! Get him below quick."

Jimmy Townsend leapt from his Browning and bent over Tom.

"How is he?" asked Harry.

"He's been hit a few times, sir. He's out cold."

"Get him below," shouted Harry.

Walter helped him to carry Tom to the wardroom.

"Bloody hell! I didn't know he'd caught it that bad. How is he?" the coxswain asked.

"Lieutenant Green is having a look at him now," replied Harry.

CHAPTER III

Wounded

They had Tom on the table in the wardroom. John was seeing to his wounds. Tom had been hit in the arm twice, and a bullet had passed straight through his left side. They gave him morphine and stopped the bleeding.

"Signal ahead and request ambulances for the wounded. Tell them ETA is in ninety minutes," said John.

"OK," said Harry. "Will he be all right?"

"I think so, but I'm not a doctor. I've done the best I can for him."

"I don't know how he kept control of the boat. He's some guy!"

With that, Harry went to the chart room to send the messages. Harry told Walter to organise some char for everyone, and to make sure he put a tot in it.

"Right, sir," replied Walter. "Come on, Jimmy – give us a hand."

"I will see to the rest of the wounded," said Harry.

"Some show that, sir!" said Jimmy. "I think I'm getting too blooming old for this lark."

"We all are," said Harry. "But I'll tell you this: we did some damage to that convoy – caught them completely by surprise."

Back in the ops room, news was coming through. The Commodore was sitting in a chair listening to the reports.

"Seems like we've given them a bloody nose," he said to his aide.

"Yes, sir."

"We've taken casualties, but we'll not know how many or how bad they are until the boats come in."

20

The Commodore was drinking his tea. He might have been a lech and not a very nice man, but he believed in looking after his men. He'd seen action in the last war, so at least he knew what it was like.

"Make sure they get those ambulances here," he said, putting down his cup. "Let's get back to HQ – they won't want us in the way. Send me a full report ASAP," he said to Marion.

"Yes, sir," she replied.

With that, he swung round and went to his waiting car.

Marion said, "Well, he isn't a saint, but when it has to be I suppose his heart's in the right place."

"Well, he knows his job," replied Lieutenant Robson. "It's just a pity he's such an arse."

Marion agreed. "I'll go and organise things for when the boats return, and I'll get them some hot food prepared; they'll be ready for some. Any news of the CO yet?"

"No," replied Lieutenant Robson. "News should start coming through any time now. I don't suppose you could organise us a brew whilst you're at it, could you? I could do with one myself after all that."

Tom came to in the hospital. He opened his eyes.

"Where the hell am I?" he asked.

"You're in hospital in Intensive Care," said Charlie. "I thought you were a goner, mate. 'How the hell am I supposed to get through this bloody war without him?' I thought. You frightened the bloody life out of me! So you just lay back and take it easy, mate. I mean, just look at all these lovely nurses around you!"

"I think I'd sooner be in the mess with you, mate," Tom replied. "I feel bloody awful. What happened?"

"You got shot, that's what happened, and you didn't even know it; you lost a lot of blood. They got the bullets out, thank God; they've done a bloody great job on you."

"Am I going to be all right?" asked Tom. "I don't want to get chucked out. Besides, I'd miss your ugly mug."

"No danger of that. Doc said you should make a full recovery – but it will take time."

"How much time?" asked Tom.

"You'll have to ask the MO that, mate, but we can't win this war without you. Besides, who's going to pull my birds for me?"

At that, the nurse came in. Charlie thought she was almost worth getting shot for.

"You will have to leave now," she said to Charlie. "He needs to rest."

"OK," he replied. "I will come back later, mate."

As he left he thought, 'God, what if he had died! I love that guy; he should get a bloody VC for what he did.'

Little did he know that Tom had been recommended for a medal by the CO, and he had also been recommended for promotion.

The nurse came round the bed now.

"Lieutenant Weston, we had better make you more comfortable," she said. "You have had a rough time."

Tom asked if she could find out how the op went against the convoy.

"Oh, I'm so sorry, but that's not my department, I'm afraid," she replied. "I'm only a nurse."

"Not *only* a nurse," Tom replied, "but thank you anyway."

She gave him an injection and he went off to sleep.

When he came to later, he could see the blackout curtains were drawn.

"Oh, you've woken up, have you?" he heard a voice say.

He turned his head and saw the CO standing there.

"Hello, sir," he said. "I am sorry about this, sir; I made a bit of a hash of things, I am afraid."

"Don't be ridiculous! You did a fine job; if it hadn't been for you and your crew, the op wouldn't have succeeded. You were spot-on with your signal."

"So the op went well?" Tom replied.

"Bloody brilliant!" the CO said. "We sank half the convoy, damaged the rest and sank three of the escorts. We only lost one of ours, and you brought the crew of that one home. How you managed it we don't know, but you did. I am recommending you for the VC and promotion."

"Good God!" Tom replied. "I can't believe it. If you don't mind me asking, sir: what about my mate, Charlie Higson?"

"Sub Lieutenant Higson has been awarded the DSO and will also be promoted. His was the boat that escorted you back to base."

"Oh, that's great, sir. I can't remember much after getting alongside; I must have passed out."

"You did. Your number one couldn't believe you got through the attack and then got your boat alongside to take the crew off. Nobody realised how badly wounded you were."

"Any idea how long I will be in dock, sir?" asked Tom.

"Yes, the doctors say it could be a couple of weeks, then a convalescent home. You will get some sick leave, then, all being well, back to duty."

"Bloody hell!" Tom blurted out. "Will I still stay with the 14th?"

"Of course you will. We can't afford to lose good men like you," the CO said.

Natalie James came into the room. "How are you, Lieutenant Weston," she asked.

"Fine, thanks," replied Tom.

"That's good," she said. "All the girls will be missing you and your friend Lieutenant Higson."

"I didn't know we were so popular."

"Oh, you would be surprised!" replied Natalie. "You are."

"Well, we will love you and leave you," the CO butted in. "Miss James and I are off to dinner with my wife and family."

"That sounds nice," said Tom. "Perhaps I might do the same one day if I ever find the right girl."

"Oh, I am sure you will," Natalie said. "Oh, if there is anything you need, just let me know."

"Thank you," answered Tom, "but Charlie will see to that."

'It must be difficult for her,' thought Tom. (He knew she was fond of the CO.) 'Ah well, that's life, I suppose. Blimey,' he thought, 'I nearly didn't see any of it!'

A doctor and a nurse came into the room.

"Well, Lieutenant Weston," the doctor said, "you are a very lucky young man. You need to take it easy for a while. I need to take some blood. How's the pain?"

"Not too bad," replied Tom. "Chest hurts a bit."

"It will do – you have some broken ribs. The nurse will get you

23

something for the pain and get you settled for the night."

With that, the doctor took the blood and left.

"What time is it?" asked Tom.

"Twenty-two hundred hours," replied the nurse.

Then the painkiller took effect and Tom dropped off to sleep.

CHAPTER IV

Plans for Christmas

The weeks went by and Tom was getting all the rest he needed. He had left the hospital and was now in the convalescent centre. It was Friday, 20 December, and the doctors had told him he could leave at the weekend. Charlie was coming to visit that afternoon. Tom thought he would ask him if he fancied going to London for a couple of weeks over Christmas and the New Year. He knew Charlie had done a couple of ops whilst he had been laid up, so he would be due for some leave.

Tom had been given his promotion and the Victoria Cross. Charlie had also got his second ring and his DSO. The investiture was to take place early in the New Year at Buckingham Palace, and they had planned a celebration afterwards.

Charlie arrived about 1400 hours.

"So how is my mate today?" asked Tom.

"Good," said Charlie, "but shouldn't I be asking you that?"

"I'm good," replied Tom. "Do you fancy a couple of weeks in town for Christmas?"

"Why not!" answered Charlie. "Where should we stay?"

"Somewhere really posh, I thought. We have loads of back pay to come."

"And why not?" Charlie agreed.

One of the guys he had met at the home was a major in the Guards. His name was Graham Yates. Tom had mentioned his idea to Graham.

"I have an uncle who is the assistant manager at the Strand Palace Hotel. I'll give him a ring and ask him if he can help you out."

"That would be great. I would be really grateful."

He told Charlie, who said he thought that would be smashing. Later in the afternoon, whilst having tea in the lounge, Graham came over to the table.

"Hi, Tom," he said.

Tom introduced Charlie, and they shook hands.

"I have rung my uncle and told him about you two. He was delighted. He said he would have a word with the manager and see what he could do. Anyway, he has just got back to me: the manager has had a word with the chairman and he said they would be honoured to have both you and your families as guests. You can have the Jubilee Suite. There's no need to worry about cost either – they are going to let you have it for free."

"Bloody hell!" they both said.

"That's great – and for nothing!" said Tom. "We would be delighted if you could come along."

"I will do my best. Just let me know the date."

"Tell you what: why don't we start our celebrations early? Let's go to the local and have a few warm-up drinks in preparation," said Tom.

"What a great idea!" said Graham. "Count me in."

After a few drinks, Charlie got the train back to base. The next morning he went to the office to sort out his leave, and he told Natalie all about it.

"Oh, that sounds wonderful!" she said.

Charlie looked at her. "I know I am being forward, but what are you doing for Christmas?"

"Nothing in particular. I don't really have any plans," she answered.

"Why don't you join us in London? I know Tom won't mind. We are staying in a suite, and there are three or four bedrooms."

Natalie looked at Charlie. "Are you sure?" she asked.

"Of course," Charlie replied. "I will give Tom a ring and let him know. I know he will be delighted."

"OK – if you're sure. I've not had a good leave for ages."

Charlie got through to Tom and told him.

Tom, as Charlie expected, was delighted.

"You couldn't get a better girl anywhere," he said.

"I shall be on my very best behaviour; Natalie is a very nice lady. We will see how it turns out."

"Well, the very best of luck to you, mate; I'll be rooting for you."

"Thanks, Tom. You're the best. Natalie is here now. Do you want a word?"

Natalie came on the line. "Hello, Tom," she said. "Thank you. I think I will enjoy myself."

"We will make sure you do. See you soon."

The familiar voice of the operator interrupted: "Your time is up, sir," she said, and the phone went dead.

Charlie looked at Natalie and said, "You don't have worry about anything, you know."

"I'm not worried," said Natalie. "I'm not a nun, you know."

"You are something special to us, you know that, don't you? Everyone on the base has a place in their hearts for you." Charlie was silent for a long moment, and then he said, "With that, I think I will go before I make a fool of myself."

He smiled as he left. He was beginning to get excited at the thought of this leave with his best friend, a pretty girl and staying at a really big posh hotel.

CHAPTER V

The Jubilee Suite

They all arrived at the Strand Palace Hotel within half an hour of one another. The manager greeted them with champagne and a little speech of welcome.

Tom replied, saying how grateful he was. He said that Charlie, his best mate, appreciated it too and added that Lieutenant Higson would be receiving a DSO at Buckingham Palace the same day.

The manager was doubly delighted and the staff applauded.

Tom said the lovely lady with them looked after everyone on the base and was a most important part of keeping the flotillas running smoothly.

Natalie blushed. She had never been praised by Tom before.

A lady was brought forward from the staff to present Tom with the key to the Jubilee Suite; she was Caroline Betson, the housekeeper. She had dark hair and was very good-looking, but there was something else about her that struck him: her eyes held him. He thought, 'This girl has a special kind of look.' He knew it was magic – no girl had made such an impression on him before. 'I must get to know this girl,' he thought.

Tom took the key.

"Will you join us for a drink later?" he asked.

She looked into his eyes and said, "I would be delighted."

This was the girl he wanted for his wife. Caroline was twenty-three and her husband was in the army in the Middle East, but before he went he had told her he had met someone else and wanted a divorce. Tom somehow felt things were going to change for the better in that moment.

Caroline's best friend, Phyllis Jones, who was the head waitress, saw the look in Tom and Caroline's eyes as they met. 'Perhaps there is such a thing as love at first sight,' she thought. She hoped so because she knew that Caroline's husband was a womaniser. They all went upstairs to the suite; Tom unlocked the door and they went in.

"Bloody hell!" Charlie exclaimed. "It's bloody marvellous!"

"It certainly is," agreed Natalie.

"Well, let's enjoy it while we can," Tom replied. "You can pick your bedrooms while I pour the champagne."

He opened the bottle and poured three glasses. "Better make that four," said Charlie. "We have company."

Caroline stood in the doorway.

"I have brought you some extra blankets just in case you need them," she said.

"Oh, thanks," said Tom. "Come and join us for a drink, won't you?"

"I can't," she replied. "I am still on duty until five o'clock."

"Will you join us later – please?" he asked.

"I would love to."

"Then we will save the other bottle until then."

"Well," Charlie said, "I think you have made an impression there."

"I hope so," replied Tom. "I think she is lovely."

"Did you notice the ring on her finger?" asked Charlie.

"I did, but I don't care – I still think she is bloody gorgeous."

At that, Natalie returned.

"Where is the lady?" she asked.

"Still working, but she is coming back later for a drink."

"Good. I think she likes you."

"Do you think so?" Tom asked.

"I do – I could see by the way she looked at you when she gave you the key."

"I hope you're right. I'm sure she is the type of girl I am looking for."

"Well, let's hope it all turns out well for you," Natalie said. "I never seem to have much luck with men."

Tom looked at her and said, "I know Charlie may not be the most sophisticated bloke you could ever meet, but he is a hell of a guy."

Natalie looked at him. "You know, you may be right, Tom. I

know he is a bit of a lad, but he has a heart of pure gold; and he would never let anyone down, that's for sure."

"So why don't you give him a chance?"

"I do find him quite attractive," she replied, "and I believe he is a sincere man, judging by some of the things he has told me about both of you. I think I should have a drink and some food before I get too philosophical. How about you?"

"I think you're right," said Tom. "I'm going to take a shower and get changed before Caroline comes back."

Charlie came back into the room.

"Hello. What are you two cooking up?" he asked.

"We were just talking about you," Tom said.

"We were saying how I should give you a chance."

"I hope you are not taking the mickey out of me," he said, looking at her.

"I'm not," she replied, "after all, you invited me."

"Yes, I did, didn't I?" he answered.

"And I accepted, didn't I?"

Charlie looked at her.

"You did! Well, I won't let you down because I respect you too much, Natalie, and a man's got to have dreams – even me," he said.

Natalie came over to him and kissed him.

"Perhaps it's not a dream," she told him. "I am not special, and I have my dreams like anyone else, so let's see how it works out, shall we?"

Tom stood listening. They both looked at him.

He winked at them and said, "I think that's bloody marvellous! The best of luck to you both! You deserve it. I am absolutely bloody over the moon for you both."

He came over to them, kissed Natalie on the cheek and shook Charlie by the hand.

"Now, that is something to drink to," he said.

"And to you and Caroline," they both replied.

Tom poured the drinks.

"Cheers!" they all said.

"It will soon be 1942, so let's hope it's a bloody good one for us all," added Charlie.

CHAPTER VI

A Happy New Year

They invited as many people as they could for a New Year's Eve party in the suite.

Tom said, "I will ask Caroline and Phyllis if they will organise the food and booze."

"Good idea!" replied Charlie.

Natalie said, "Charlie and I will go into town and get some decorations to put about the suite."

Natalie and Charlie were getting along just great.

"That's settled, then," Tom replied. "Let's make it a good one because we don't know what the next twelve months may bring."

They all looked at one another, knowing that it could be a dangerous year.

Caroline came up to the suite. She had finished work.

"Hello," said Tom. "You look tired."

"I am," she said, "but the manager has given me time off till you go back so we can be together."

"Oh, that's good of him."

"Can we sit down? There is something I want to tell you."

"OK," he answered, "but let's have a brew first."

"You and your brews!" said Caroline.

"I know," replied Tom, "but it's the only thing that keeps me going sometimes. Right, my love, tell me – I am all ears."

"Well, darling, as you may have guessed from this ring, I am married."

"Yes," he replied, "but I don't care. I didn't say anything because I knew you would tell me in your own time."

"Thank you," Caroline replied. She told him the whole story.

Tom took her hands in his and said, "Sweetheart, I am still young, but I have seen many awful things in my life and perhaps that has made me callous; the way I see it is, he left you, which means now I can have you all to myself. I know that I love you very much, and I won't ever let you down or ever let you go."

She had tears in her eyes. "Oh, Tom," she said, "I love you more than anyone in the world, and I never want to lose you ever. I know you have to leave soon, and I am so scared."

"Don't be," said Tom. "Before I just did my job – a bit devil-may-care, I know – but now I have someone and something to live for. I know it's early days, but I want you to be my wife."

"Oh, Tom, I want that too – more than anything else in the whole world. You promise me you will be careful."

"Don't worry," he replied, "that will be my first priority. Besides, Charlie wants a double wedding."

"Oh," she cried, "that would be really something, but I have to wait for my decree absolute to come through."

"That's all right," Tom replied with a wink; "I am a patient man now."

"I am so happy we have sorted that out. I said to Phyllis, 'I hoped this works out for me.' "

"Have I met her?" asked Tom.

"No," said Caroline, "but you saw her when I gave you the key."

"Ah, the good-looking girl with the blonde hair; I remember. Will you invite her to our shindig – and her boyfriend if she has one?"

"She hasn't got one. She was let down a while back."

"Well, we will have to see if we can remedy that," replied Tom.

"That would be nice, darling."

"That's settled, then," he said. "I want to make love to you now, sweetheart."

"I thought you would never ask," replied Caroline with a smile on her face.

He took her hand and led her into the bedroom.

Charlie and Natalie came into the suite.

"They must have gone out," Charlie said.

"I don't think so," replied Natalie. "Can't you hear that? I think it gives it away, don't you."

"Oh," said Charlie, "I think you're right. Shall we retire gracefully?"

She took his hand. "Not too gracefully, I hope," she said with a giggle as she led him into their bedroom.

Some time later they were all sitting in the cocktail bar waiting for Phyllis, whom Caroline had asked to join them for a drink.

"Here she comes!" Caroline said.

"My word," said Tom and Charlie together, "now, that is glamour!"

Phyllis came over. "Thank you for the invitation," she said.

"Our pleasure!" they both replied.

"You look wonderful. I can see we will have to keep an eye on these two," said Caroline.

"We will indeed," agreed Natalie. "But, Phyllis, you do look really lovely."

"I am usually all dressed up with nowhere to go. That's the story of my life these days," said Phyllis.

"You must have the boys falling all over you," said Tom.

"Oh, that will be the day!" she replied. "It would be very nice to get a bit of attention."

She sat down.

Charlie asked, "What are you having?"

"Can I have a cocktail, please?"

"You can have anything you want," replied Charlie.

The night went really well. They all got to know Phyllis.

Before she left to get her taxi, Tom said, "You are coming to the big party, aren't you?"

"Oh yes. I just wish I had someone nice to bring."

"Well, you never know – something good might happen," said Tom.

"Oh, I wish it would."

They all saw her out into the street, where a taxi was waiting, and Caroline gave her a big hug.

As she got into the taxi she said, "Whatever happens I will still enjoy myself."

"That's the spirit!" said Charlie, and Natalie added, "We will make sure you do."

Caroline gave her a kiss. "Don't worry, love," she whispered. "I know you will have a good time."

"Oh, Caroline, I am so happy for you to have found someone like Tom!"

When Phyllis left they went back to the suite.

"She is very nice. I hope she meets someone," said Natalie.

"So do I, but we have more important things to think about now."

"I wonder what that could be," said Caroline.

"Don't tease me," said Tom, smacking her on the bottom.

With that, they said goodnight and went into their room. Tom took her in his arms.

"I want you take me now. I want you to undress me," she said.

Tom looked at her naked body and said, "I have never seen anything so lovely in my life."

They fell on to the bed and began to make love.

The New Year's party went with a bang. Everybody there seemed to enjoy it. Some of the hotel staff came with their wives and girlfriends. Graham arrived with his wife – a very glamorous actress – and they brought a couple of friends. It was a shame that none of the crews were able to make it, but they had their own families and friends to party with. They let the New Year in. Tom and Caroline, Charlie and Natalie and Phyllis held hands and sang 'Auld Lang Syne'.

Tom looked over at Phyllis, who had tears streaming down her face. 'Hell!' he thought, 'I wish we could have found someone for her.'

Suddenly the doors were flung open and in walked John Green, Tom's navigator.

"Good God!" cried Tom. "Where the hell have you come from?" he asked, grasping John's hand.

"I was at my mum's and I thought I would come and see you. So I grabbed a cab from Pinner and here I am."

"And a sight for sore eyes too!" said Tom.

John looked at Phyllis and asked, "Who is this gorgeous creature? She's an angel."

"Allow me to present this angel to you. This is Miss Phyllis Jones, and, Miss Jones, this is Lieutenant John Green, DSO, my navigator and bachelor in His Majesty's Royal Navy."

Phyllis looked at John and smiled. "I don't think I have ever seen such a handsome man in my life." She took his arm. "You are mine," she said.

"You really are an angel sent from heaven above for me, and I won't let you escape," he replied.

"I don't think I want to," she said, and with that she put her arms around his neck and kissed him full on the lips.

"What a way to let in the New Year!" said Tom.

Charlie picked up a bottle of champagne, opened it, got six glasses and filled them. They held up their drinks and downed them in one.

"Happy New Year, darling," said Tom.

"And to you," Caroline replied. "You really are a lovely man. I have never felt so happy in my whole life. Here's to the four of us – and long may it last."

'The beginning of 1942 is a good one,' thought Tom. 'Long may it go on.'

CHAPTER VII

The Luckiest Two Guys in the World

After saying goodbye to Caroline at the station, they boarded the train back to base. Charlie and Natalie sat holding hands, and Tom settled back into his seat. He closed his eyes and thought of all that had happened over the last two weeks. So much had changed; things would never be the same again. Being in love was the most tremendous feeling he had ever had, and life felt really good. He knew that Charlie and Natalie felt the same. He also knew that after his check-up, if everything was OK (which he hoped it would be), he would have to go back to the war.

Natalie said to Charlie, "Who would have thought this would ever happen to us?"

"Yes," he replied, "but it has and I am so pleased. I never thought I could be so in love."

"Oh, my darling Charlie, I am so glad. I feel the same way about you, but at least I will be near you most of the time. I know I won't be on ops, but I will be there for you when you return."

"That will make it a lot easier for me, sweetheart," he replied.

It took about two and half hours to get back to Harwich. When they arrived it had started to snow.

"That's all we need!" said Charlie.

"Well, here we are. Didn't the time fly? When do you go for your check-up?" asked Natalie.

"In a couple of days," Tom answered. "I hope they let me get back to duty."

"I wouldn't be in too much of a hurry to get back to the war. Just make sure you're fit," said Charlie.

"Oh, I will do that," replied Tom.

"Anyway, you will be able to help out in the ops room," added Natalie, "and I can pop in and keep you company."

"Well, I wouldn't grumble at that," Tom replied.

"Aye, and you will be able to keep an eye on her for me," said Charlie.

"Cheeky thing!" she replied.

"You know I'm only kidding, love."

"I know, sweet."

"Well, come on, you two," Tom said. "They will be taking us back to London if we don't get a move on."

"We wouldn't complain about that too much," Natalie answered. "Anyway, we will all be going back shortly – I wonder if there is any word about the date yet."

"It should be soon," replied Charlie. "The wagon's here – let's get on. It's bloody freezing."

As the wagon pulled in through the gate, Natalie said, "Hey, look – they are turning out the guard. There must be someone important coming."

"Better get out of the way," Charlie said.

Tom noticed that Dave Hill was leading the guard out. "They've got my coxswain leading the guard," Tom said.

"Bloody hell! I've never seen him look so smart," Charlie retorted.

They got out of the wagon and the CO came across.

Dave shouted, "Present arms!"

"What's all this?" asked Tom.

"It's for you, Lieutenant Weston. A holder of the Victoria Cross always receives a special reception."

Tom's mouth dropped open. "Well, I never! For me? Blimey, sir!"

"Well, you had better go over and inspect the guard."

Tom strode over. It was snowing hard, but he didn't seem to notice it.

The coxswain threw up a smart salute and said, "Welcome back, sir. It's good to see you."

"It's good to be back and to see you too," replied Tom. "What a cracking turnout! Thank you."

With that the CO shouted, "Three cheers!"

"Hip hip hooray! Hip hip hooray! Hip hip hooray!" they all shouted.

Tom blushed, but he felt so proud; Charlie and Natalie looked on.

"That's my best mate," said Charlie with obvious affection. "Makes you feel fair proud, don't it?"

Natalie looked at him and thought, 'It must be wonderful to have a friend like that with not a bad thought in him – and he is all mine. I never thought I could be so lucky.'

She put her arm through his. "Come on, darling," she said. "Let's go and congratulate him."

They went across to Tom.

"Well done, Tom," they said as they shook his hand.

The CO turned and said, "Oh, by the way: you are on the same day, Lieutenant Higson – March 14th, 1100 hours. Now let's get out of this bloody snow and go and have a drink in the mess. I am going numb with cold."

Later, as they sat in their room, Charlie said, "That was really something, wasn't it?"

"Certainly was!" replied Tom. "I never expected anything like that."

"Ah well," Charlie replied, "it will be back to the old routine soon, mate."

"It will be for you; and I hope it's not too long before I get back into the swing of things again too."

"I suppose so," Charlie replied, "but it won't be quite the same any more. No more saunters into town looking for a nice lady!"

"Hey, you're not complaining, I hope!" Tom exclaimed.

"No, I'm not. We must be the luckiest two guys in the world. I mean: medals, promotion and a wonderful girl each," he replied. "Things can't get much better, can they?"

"Not likely, I shouldn't think!" Tom replied. "We'll have a drink to that later. Now I must go and try to book a call to Caroline. I want to give her the good news."

CHAPTER VIII

Back to Work

They had been back two weeks. Charlie had been on a couple of ops, but the bad weather had curtailed ops for a while. Tom had his check-up and was passed fit for duty, much to his pleasure. He was now on 326, checking things over with John Green.

"It's good to have you back, skip," John said. "Harry did a fine job while you were off, but he couldn't wait for you to take over again."

"Thanks," replied Tom. "I'm glad to get back on board again. Oh, by the way, how are you and Phyllis getting along?"

"Oh, just great," John said. "We have decided to get engaged."

"Well, that's bloody marvellous news, John. Nineteen forty-two is turning out to be a good year for us all."

"Seems like that. I never thought it would happen to me in a million years," he responded, "but I'm over the moon it has."

In the mess that evening they were all having a drink together to celebrate John's good news.

Charlie said, "Looks as though we will be off ops until this freeze is over."

"It won't be all that long, according to the weather reports coming through. It should clear within forty-eight hours, so the Met boys say," said John.

Natalie came into the mess and went over to the table. "What's the celebration?" she asked.

"John and Phyllis are getting engaged," Tom said.

"Oh, that's wonderful!" She kissed John on the cheek. "You are a lucky man," she said.

"I know," replied John. "I feel like I am walking on air."

"Have you heard from Caroline?" she asked Tom.

"Yes. She is coming down this weekend," he replied.

"That's good news," Charlie said, "that's if there are no ops."

"There won't be, not until after the weekend," she said.

"Great!" said Charlie.

"It's nice to have someone in the know," said John.

"Certainly is," Tom replied. "It means I can make plans. God, I can't wait to see her again!"

"You are a lucky blighter," he said to his mate. "Well, you will have to get Caroline to join the Wrens, won't you, mate?"

They all laughed.

"Well, I will get another round in," Charlie offered.

They stayed in the mess until about 2300 hours,

"Come on, love – we will love you and leave you all," said Charlie. "We will go to our secret little place, Nat."

"OK," replied Tom. "See you later, mate. You are a lucky blighter, you know. Anyway, I will try to ring Caroline and wish her goodnight."

"Give her a big kiss from us if you get through," said Natalie.

"I will do, if I get through."

Natalie gave Tom a kiss. "You will be seeing each other soon anyway," she said.

With that, Natalie and Charlie left.

Tom ordered another gin and went off to try to phone Caroline. To his surprise, he got through straight away.

"Oh, darling," she cried, "it's so good to hear your voice, sweetheart. I miss you so much."

"I miss you too, my sweet, but we will soon be together. There are no ops, so I'm going to book us the best room at the Metropole Hotel for the weekend."

"I can't wait to get my arms around you again, my love," said Caroline. "I'm going to lock the door so you can't get out. It will be so good."

The operator's voice said, "Sorry, your time's up," and the phone went dead.

"Bloody hell!" Tom muttered. "It's always the bloody same: we just get to the interesting part and the damn phone goes dead."

He finished his drink and went off to his room. It was snowing heavily and freezing cold. 'I hope the bloody boiler is working and the room is warm,' he thought.

Natalie and Charlie were as warm as toast in each other's arms. They were in a little warm corner of the boiler room.

Natalie murmured, "Oh, Charlie, take me, darling, please" – and he did.

Tom was reading when Charlie arrived back.

"Hey," he said, "everything all right?"

"Couldn't be better," Charlie replied with a gleam in his eye.

"You lucky sod – having your girlfriend on base," he said.

"I know. Did you get through to her?"

"Yeah," Tom replied, "I got through straight away. She is fine, and she says she can't wait to get here."

"That's good. What are you reading?" Charlie asked.

"Sherlock Holmes," said Tom.

"I never got into reading," replied Charlie.

"You should give it a try sometime. It's good for relaxing you – especially after heavy exercise," Tom said with a smile.

"Oh, right! I will have to try it sometime. I am hoping to get a lot of heavy exercise in the future."

"Cheeky!" said Tom. "Good on you, mate."

"I think I'll borrow one of your books sometime."

"Help yourself," said Tom.

"OK. I'm off for my shower," Charlie replied. "You should get some kip."

"I'm just going to read another couple of chapters and then get my head down. I plan to do some work on 326."

"I'll be doing the same on 324," Charlie replied. "If this weather clears, we'll be getting busy again."

The weekend came and went. Tom and Caroline had a great time together. He showed her round his boat, and she was fascinated and so pleased to see where he worked. Afterwards he saw her off on the train.

Tom gave her a great big hug and said, "Have a good journey.

I'll see you soon." He then told her the date of his investiture.

"Oh, that will be really something to look forward to. I'll have to get myself a new outfit; I must look my best for you."

"For the occasion," Tom replied. "You always look great to me. We'll have a great time, Caroline."

"When you've got your medal, I'm going to take you to bed and lock the bedroom door."

"Is that a threat or a promise," asked Tom.

"It's a promise," she replied.

"You are getting very cheeky," he replied.

"I know, but it's you who has made me that way."

"That's good. I'll see you soon," Tom said.

"You will. Take care of yourself!"

"I will. Jerry isn't going to get me."

CHAPTER IX

Secert Mission

Tom was working on the boat when a leading seaman came over and said, "The CO would like to see you in his office, sir."

"Righto," Tom answered. "I will come right away."

"What was that about?" asked Charlie.

"I don't know," replied Tom. "The CO wants to see me."

"Could be an op!"

"I'll find out soon."

Tom knocked on the office door, and a voice said, "Come in."

"Hello, Nat. The CO sent for me. Is he in?"

"Yes. Go right in."

"Thanks. Do you know if it's about an op?"

"I think so," Natalie replied.

Tom knocked on the door and went in.

"Ah, Lieutenant Weston! Take a seat. We have a job for you."

"What is it, sir?" asked Tom.

"Make yourself comfortable and I will tell you as much as I know." He rang through to the outer office: "Can you organise some tea, please?"

"Right away, sir," Natalie replied. "I will bring it through to you."

"Thank you," he replied.

They waited until Natalie brought the tea and left the office.

"Now, Tom, this is the operation – well, as much as I can tell you. You will cross the Channel to Holland to drop some SOE agents at a designated spot."

"Yes, sir," said Tom.

"That's not all," replied the CO: "you will then pick up some Dutch

43

operatives from another rendezvous point and bring them back. We know it could be – and most probably will be – dangerous," he said. "We needed an experienced skipper and crew, so I have selected you."

"Right, sir. We will do our best," he replied.

"There is something you must know," the CO said: "Harry has reported sick. The Chief Medical Officer thinks it's pneumonia."

"Jesus! He said he felt groggy this morning in the mess. Will he be all right?"

"The MO has sent him to hospital. You will need a new number one. Do you have anyone in mind?"

"Yes, sir – my mate Charlie."

"I thought you would say that, so I checked the roster and you're in luck."

"That's great, sir," replied Tom. "He is working on his boat, so I can tell him when I get back."

"These two envelopes contain all the information you will need, but you must not open the second one until you are at sea."

"Right, sir." Tom stood up. "I will get back to the boat. Oh, thank you for the tea."

He left the office.

"Well? Is it an op?" Natalie asked.

"Yes," Tom said. "We've got to take some SOE agents over to Holland and bring some people back tomorrow night. There's just one slight problem, though."

"What's that?"

"Harry has been taken to hospital."

"Oh, God!" Natalie cried. "Is he all right?"

"At the moment," Tom replied, "but I need a replacement number one."

"Charlie?"

"Yes. I hope you don't mind."

"You know I don't – you couldn't get a better man, and we hadn't made any plans. Does he know yet?"

"No, not yet. I'm going to tell him now," Tom replied.

"Do you mind if I come with you?" she asked.

"No, not at all. I'll be glad of the company."

"I'll get my coat," she said. "At least it's stopped snowing."

"It's not too bad now," Tom said, "but it's still bloody cold. We can wrap up against it."

"Oh, that reminds me," said Natalie, reaching into her desk drawer: "I have knitted these for you. Hope you like them."

She handed him two parcels.

"Thanks. I am sure we will."

They walked down to the quay together. When they found Charlie, he was talking to his number one.

"Hello," he said. "I hope you are not pinching my girl."

"Never!" replied Natalie.

"I'm pinching you for a job," said Tom.

"Oh yes? What job is that?"

"Before I tell you, let's open these," Tom said, handing him his parcel.

They both opened them together. Inside were two navy-blue knitted scarves.

"Excellent!" they both cried.

"I just wanted to make sure your necks were nice and warm. I'm glad you like them," she said.

"I didn't know you were so talented, my love," said Charlie.

He put his arms around her and gave her a big kiss, and Tom kissed her on the cheek and said thank you. Tom then told Charlie about Harry.

"Let's hope he will be OK," said Charlie, "but I am pleased we've got the chance to work together, mate."

Natalie looked at them. She said, "I pity the Germans now, having to take on you two together."

"Those two could take on the world and beat it," said Alan.

Natalie thought, 'They are the most liked guys anyone could ever know. I feel so proud to know them.'

"OK, now are you going to tell me what the job is?" he asked Tom.

"If you come on board, I will give you the details."

Natalie said, "I had better get back to the office or the CO will think I have gone on my holidays. See you both later."

Off she went, and Tom and Charlie went on board 326. Tom asked his coxswain, Dave, to organise a brew and then join them in the wardroom with Lieutenant Green.

They sat round the wardroom table.

"Good drop of char this," Charlie remarked. "You must give my lads some lessons on making tea, Chief. Ours always tastes like bilge water, but don't tell them I said so."

Tom opened the first envelope to start the briefing.

"The op is tomorrow night at 2100 hours. Two SOE agents will arrive. It's our job to get them across the Channel to Holland and drop them at a point just up the coast from a fishing village called Volendam. Now, we have been told that there are E-boats and armed trawlers stationed there. If all goes well, we then proceed to a pickup point, where we will pick up two Dutch boffins, a father and daughter who, it seems, are quite important people. Everything must be kept tight. John, these are the signals, course and position of minefields for you to study and digest. I know it sounds easy, but we all know it is never as easy as it looks. With German units in the area, we will have to be extremely alert at all times – but I don't need to remind you all of that. Now, we will have to rely on the Dutch to be on time. We must get those boffins on board and away at all costs. I am going to need three guys, armed and ready to go ashore to help them out of any trouble – nothing gung-ho and no heroics."

Dave said, "I can sort out a landing party, sir, if you want me to."

"Thanks. I will leave that to you, then."

"Do you want me to go ashore?" asked Charlie.

"No, I bloody don't!" said Tom. "I want you on the wheel in case we have to get the hell out of it bloody quick."

Tom finished the briefing. "That's as much as I can tell you right now. Oh, Dave, will you let the boys in the engine room know, and tell them I will give them all a quick briefing to put them in the picture. There will be no shore runs tonight; this has got to have the lid kept tight. Any questions? Nothing? Right, we will finish off the boat and call it a day. Thank you, gentlemen."

"Can I say anything to my lads?" asked Charlie.

"Yes," Tom said. "It's only fair they know what their skip's up to, but keep it to the bare essentials."

"OK, I will just have a quick word; then I'm off to have a shower. Catch you later, mate," said Charlie. "I'll meet you in the mess for something to eat and a couple of drinks; then I'll have an early night, I think."

"Not too early, mate," Tom replied. "We're not on till tomorrow night."

"Oh, right. I will spend a bit of time with Nat, then."

Tom and Charlie were talking to the CO, waiting for the SOE agents to arrive.

"They should be here any time now," said the CO.

As he was speaking, a pair of headlights came through the gates and down the quay. "This will be them."

The car stopped and the driver jumped out; he opened the rear door and two people emerged.

The CO said, "Have a good journey?"

"Same as all the others," came the curt reply.

Charlie said, "He sounds a barrel of laughs, doesn't he?"

Another voice, female this time, said, "Sorry about that, but he has a lot on his mind."

"We all have that problem," said Tom. "Anyway, we had better get on board."

The two passengers were taken to the wardroom.

"Right, we had better get under way."

Dave signalled the engine room to start the engines. He eased the throttles open, and the boat slid away from the quay and gathered speed.

"Come on – let's go to the chart room, mate," said Tom.

John Green was already in there looking at the charts and signal pads.

"Everything OK?" Charlie asked.

"Yes, all OK," answered John.

"Right, now we have cleared the harbour we can open the other envelope up and see what is in it."

Tom tore it open and read the contents in silence.

"You had better have a look at these for yourselves," he said.

They both had a good look at the contents.

"Bloody hell!" Charlie exclaimed.

"That's a surprise," John said. "Well, I think I have heard everything now. I can now see why they wanted a landing party."

"Yes," Tom replied, "there could be trouble if he is to get awkward. Anyway, we will have a talk with the landing party."

47

A little later the two mates were stood on the bridge.

"Well, there is one thing in our favour," Charlie said: "It's nice and dark, so we have good cover."

"It's a good job it is, mate," replied Tom. "Will you go round the boat and make sure everything is OK? Then join us in the wardroom."

"Right, skip. Will do."

"It's strange hearing you saying that," said Tom before he left the bridge.

The tiny wardroom was a bit crowded when Charlie got back.

Tom looked around. "I know it's a wee bit tight in here," he said.

"Quite snug really," said George Davies, one of the landing party.

"You will set people talking, George, saying things like that," said Bill Roe.

There was laughter all round – even the two agents from SOE joined in.

"OK," said Tom, "having just read the rest of the orders, I thought it only fair that the landing party should know what's in store for them."

"Thanks very much, sir," they all replied.

"Well, here goes," he began: "as you already know, we have to drop off our two friends here in Holland and then go to the next point to pick up some important boffins and take them back to base. Now listen very carefully: the two boffins are father and daughter, which is OK, but the other person – and listen to this – is the daughter's boyfriend. That's not unusual, you may think, but she insists she will not leave him at any cost. We can all understand that, except in this case the boyfriend is a major in the German Army and, understandably, he doesn't want to come. So the plan is to drug him heavily and bring him out that way."

"Well, if he wakes up," Bill said, "it would give me great pleasure to put him to sleep again – *permanently*."

"Now then, Bill! He will be a prisoner of war and under the protection of the Geneva Convention."

"The Geneva Convention my arse!" Bill replied. "I would still put him to sleep permanently."

"You are a very nasty young man," said George.

"Not so much of the *young*, mate," he said.

"OK," interjected Tom, "that's how it stands, so we will see how it turns out."

The meeting ended and they went back to their stations.

The young lady said to Tom, "With men like that fighting for us, there is no way we can lose this war."

"They are a bit rough around the edges, but they're one hell of a crew and I'm proud as hell of them. I would lay my life down defending any of them."

"It's wonderful to hear an officer say that about his men."

Tom thanked her and went back to the bridge.

"What a fine commanding officer he is!" said the young girl.

"He is," replied her companion, "but have you noticed what he wears on his chest?"

"No," she said.

"Well, he wears the ribbon of the DSC and, more importantly, the ribbon of the Victoria Cross."

"Oh, my word!" she exclaimed. "No wonder his crew really look up to him!"

"Well, there aren't many like him around. Like you said, with men like them on our side there is no way we can lose this war, no matter how long it takes."

On the bridge, Charlie was talking to the coxswain.

"Everything OK?" Tom asked.

"Fine. Course 242, speed 22 knots, sir," the coxswain said.

"Good. I think it's time for a brew with a drop of something in it," Charlie said.

"Will you see to that, Chief? I will take over the wheel."

"Right, sir," replied the coxswain.

Tom said, "Got any ideas, mate?"

Charlie thought for a while until the coxswain brought them a brew. "I have sent one round the boat, sir," he said.

"OK," Tom replied. "Could you do me a big favour and put the engine-room boys in the picture?"

"Yes, sir. I will do that now." With that he left the bridge.

Lieutenant Green came up to the bridge.

"I have checked the radio and charts," he said.

"Everything OK?" asked Tom.

"Yes," he replied. "The only problem is if our major happens to come too. He doesn't know we know about the German units at Volendam, and I'm thinking they will only be a problem if they are alerted to what is going on."

"Yes, you're right," Tom replied.

"So when we get the landing party ashore," said Charlie, "if the Dutch are on the pier ready to go, there shouldn't be a problem."

"That sounds sensible to me," replied John. "After all, we will have to deal with whatever happens at the time."

"OK," answered Tom, "we will proceed and take it from there. Thank you for your views. Are you all happy to carry on? The only other thing is that this German major might have alerted his superiors to the fact that there is a plan afoot to spirit his girlfriend and her father out of the country."

"I can see your point," Charlie said, "but we will just have to get on with the bloody job and take it as it comes."

"As long as we all stay alert – and I know we will – everything should go according to plan."

"Well, I have got everything crossed," replied John.

They all had a little chuckle.

"Well, let's get on with it, then," said Tom. "Can we go to the chart room, John, and take a look at the charts?"

"OK, sir."

In the chart room they went over the maps of the area.

John pointed out the minefields and said, "There are some tricky currents along this stretch of coast, but the weather is good for us. The forecast is for light winds and later snow showers, which should help to cover any engine noise."

"Good – we need all the help we can get," said Tom. "Our heads are on the bloody chopping block if it goes wrong."

"I don't think we will have to worry too much about that. We will all be either dead or captured."

"Thanks for that! What a cheerful thought!" Tom replied. "But you're right. We'll just have to make sure it doesn't go wrong, then."

CHAPTER XI

In Enemy Waters

Everyone on the boat was fully alert; all the guns had been tested and were loaded, cocked and ready.

Todd Soames on the Bofors gun said to Les Wright, "If we meet any E-boats, we had better shoot straighter than we have ever done before or we'll be in deep shit."

"Aye," replied Les, "up to our bloody necks!"

Tom and Charlie were on the bridge. The coxswain was in the engine room updating them with everything that was happening.

Yorkie Cowling said, "OK, Reg, we had better make sure we can give the skipper everything he asks for."

"Too bloody right!" he replied. "I don't fancy ending up dead or captured."

"Don't be so bloody pessimistic," said the coxswain. "The skipper will get us through this – you know he will."

"Aye, we know that," Yorkie answered. "We can always rely on him."

Tom looked at his watch. "Ten minutes to go," he said.

"OK," replied Charlie. "Do you want me to take over?"

"Yes please, mate," replied Tom. "I will go and get the passengers on deck, ready to go."

With that Charlie took the wheel and they shook hands.

"It will be OK," said Charlie.

"I know it will. It's good to have you with me."

"Thanks, mate. We will sort the bastards out if they show up."

They were coming up to the drop point.

"Watch for the signal. It should be off the starboard bow about now."

Tom brought the two SOE agents on deck.

"Any time now," he said to them. At that, he saw two sharp flashes. "That's it," he said. "As soon as the dinghy comes alongside, get in as quick as you can."

He shook hands with them both.

"Thanks," the girl said.

"Sorry for seeming so rude earlier," the man said.

"Forget it," replied Tom. "You are very brave people."

At that, they jumped into the dinghy and were soon out of sight in the darkness.

'Rather them than me!' Tom thought.

"Well, Dave, that's the first part taken care of; now comes the tricky bit."

"It might not turn out to be as tricky as we think," said Dave.

"Let's hope not," Tom replied.

Back on the bridge, Charlie pushed open the throttles as soon as he got the all-clear. The boat shot smoothly forward, gathering speed. 'So far, so good!' he thought. There was a swell running, but 326 ran through it easily.

Lieutenant Green came on to the bridge.

"Nothing on the set," he said.

"Good," Charlie replied.

On the forward cannon, Bob Crowe said to his mate, "Can you hear something?"

"Don't know," Stan replied.

"Um," Bob said, "I think I will go forward and have a listen." He went up into the bows and strained his ears. "Yes, there is something out there," he said to himself. He went to the cannon, stood on the ammo locker and shouted, "I think I can hear something out there, sir."

Tom shouted, "Right, I will come down."

He went forward with Bob, and they both listened.

"I think you are right," he said. "Well done!"

"Sounds like a diesel, sir," Bob replied. "It could be an E-boat or a trawler."

"Good man!" Tom said. "You have done well."

"Thank you, sir. Right, we'd better get on the cannon; we might be needed."

Tom got back to the bridge.

"Something out there to port seems to be running on a similar course to us. It's a good job we have the dark to cover us."

John Green came up to the bridge.

"What is happening?" he asked.

"There's a boat on a similar course to us off to port," answered Charlie.

John replied, "It could be a patrol boat heading back home."

"Let's cut the engine and see what happens," said Tom. "Can you nip round the boat and ask everyone to stand by."

John rushed off, the engine was cut and they stood and listened.

Charlie said, "It seems to be pulling away from us."

They continued to listen. John came back to the bridge. It was very tense.

"If he is heading back to Volendam, that's about ten miles away," said John.

"Right, we will drift for a while – see how it goes," Tom answered.

"I don't think they could have heard us, mate," Charlie said to Tom.

"It seems not," Tom said. "We will let him put some distance between us then make for the next pickup point."

"That was bloody scary!" Todd said to his mate.

The engine of the other boat, whatever it was, couldn't be heard now.

"Do you think we are OK now?" Tom asked Charlie.

"I think so," he replied.

"OK, let's move. We have ten minutes to make it."

The engine was started up, Charlie eased the throttles open and 326 moved smoothly forward.

"Do you want to take her?" he asked.

"No," Tom replied, "I want you on the wheel. We may need a bloody fast getaway. Hopefully I will be on the pier getting our guests on board."

"OK," Charlie replied. "Let's hope it all goes off nice and smoothly."

The coxswain came to the bridge.

"Landing party ready, skip," he shouted.

He was armed with a Tommy gun and a couple of grenades. He went back to the side.

"Come on, lads – let's get ready to go."

George Davies and Bill Roe both had Sten guns and grenades. They were ready to jump ashore; they waited tensely for the signal from the pier.

"There it is," shouted Lieutenant Green.

Tom shouted, "Take her in, Charlie."

Charlie throttled back and glided in to the pier smoothly.

Tom shouted "Any trouble?" to the Browning crew.

"Open up," Charlie shouted, "and be bloody careful – don't hit any of our lot."

He could make out the people stood on the pier as he brought 326 to a standstill.

"Well done! Let's get down there," Tom shouted.

A voice in English said, "Glad to see you lot. We have the boffins and a sleeping Jerry here."

"We were bloody lucky – we just dodged a German patrol. I think they're heading this way, so we had better be as quick as we can. Right, coxswain, take the lads up the pier a bit and give us covering fire if need be. There are some barrels just up there and they will give you some cover."

"I think I will go with them," said Lieutenant Green.

"OK," yelled Tom, "but no heroics! As soon as we are loaded, get back; the guns on the boat should be able to keep them off."

They got the two boffins on board and were lifting the major when the daughter shouted, "Please be careful with him."

Tom yelled, "To hell with that! Just get him on board. I won't risk my crew for anybody."

With that, she went silent.

"If it was left to me, I would chuck him in the bleeding drink."

They suddenly heard firing up ahead.

"That bloody Jerry patrol must be coming."

They heard explosions; then the coxswain and John came running back carrying one of the crew. They got him on to the deck with the rest of the landing party.

"Open fire!" shouted Tom. "Give the bastards all you have got."

The Bofors gun and the Brownings opened up.

"How many?" yelled Tom.

"Couple of dozen," John yelled. "We got three or four of them."

Having made sure everyone was back on board, Charlie pushed the throttles open and swung 326 away from the pier.

"Cease firing," shouted Tom.

Once they were facing out to sea, they gathered speed until they were approaching forty knots.

"Well done, mate!" Tom said as he came on to the bridge. "Thanks for getting us out of that bloody hole."

"All part of the service, skip," Charlie replied, "but it was a bloody close-run thing, I think."

"You can say that again! But the lads were bloody brilliant as usual."

The coxswain came up to the bridge from the wardroom, where they had taken the wounded crewman.

"Who got wounded?" asked Tom.

"Bill Roe," he replied.

"Is it bad?" asked Charlie.

"In the chest."

"Bloody sod it!" Tom shouted, banging his fist down hard.

"Will he be OK?" asked Charlie.

"The Lieutenant is working on him now, sir," replied Dave. "He has stopped the bleeding. The girl is helping him. Well, actually it's the other way round: he is helping her. Apparently she is a doctor."

"Well, let's hope she is a good one," said Tom.

"She seems to know what she is doing."

The boat was tearing along now.

"Better ease her down a bit, mate," said Tom. "Give the doctor a steady platform to work on."

Charlie shut the throttles down, and 326 eased back to a steady twenty knots.

"We should be out of trouble by now."

It was starting to snow lightly.

"This snow should help reduce visibility too."

"Yes, and it should help to muffle the engine noise," the coxswain said.

"We should be back at base by first light if it doesn't get any worse than this," said Charlie.

The girl came up to the bridge, her jumper and trousers covered in blood. Tom looked at her.

"I'm sorry about shouting at you earlier," he said.

"Oh, that's all right," she replied. "I don't blame you. It must be difficult for you to understand how I could be in love with a German officer, but he really isn't a typical Nazi. In fact, he isn't a Nazi at all."

"If you say so, but I wasn't prepared to put my crew at risk for him or anyone else."

"But that is what you did in the line of duty. I suppose it's funny how people see things in different ways. Your crewman is sleeping now; he will be all right as long as he is kept still. I couldn't get all the bullets out, but he will be OK; he still needs to get to hospital as soon as possible. My father and I thank you for all you have done for us. You and your crew are brave men."

"That's all right. It's all part of the service – but thank you for that."

Two hours later they were back at base. Reg had gone off to hospital, and the two boffins and the major had been whisked off to some secret destination. Tom and Charlie were in the office with the CO, drinking large mugs of tea laced with whiskey while they gave their report.

"Well done again!" the CO said. "I knew you would pull it off."

"Thanks to a bloody good crew, sir – and a special thanks to Charlie for all the help he gave me. What will happen to the German, sir?" Tom asked.

"He is some kind of chemist, so I suppose they will find him a suitable job – that is, if he decides to co-operate with us. But that is their problem. Apparently, he isn't all bad: he saved them from being sent to a labour camp."

"Is that all, sir?" Tom asked.

"Yes – dismiss," said the CO.

With that, Tom stood up and said, "Well, mate, let's go eat and get some sleep; it's been a hard two days."

"And I don't suppose it will be the last of them," replied Charlie.

CHAPTER XII

New Uniforms

In the weeks after the trip to Volendam Charlie and Tom both completed more ops, though none were quite as hairy as the one they had done together. Now the time for the investiture was drawing near. Charlie and Natalie decided to get engaged; Tom and Caroline had had a couple of weekends together.

"When you come up to receive your medal," she told him, "I should have some good news about my divorce. The solicitors have told me that the decree nisi should come through soon."

"Good show!" he exclaimed. "We will be able to make some plans for the future."

Caroline had asked Tom not to rush her into everything too quickly.

"Don't get me wrong," she said: "I still want you so much, but you see, darling, I never had a proper courtship when I got married, and I really would like us to have the romance and everything else I feel I missed before."

"My darling, I shall romance you and love you and I will never ever let you down. I love and respect you with all my heart, and I would rather die than do anything to lose you," replied Tom.

"Oh, sweetheart, I know that everything will be perfect for us."

Tom returned to base and completed one more op taking agents to Holland, this time without any trouble.

The CO sent for him and Charlie.

"Sit down," he said. "Make yourselves comfortable."

They looked at each other, then at the CO.

"Oh, don't worry," he said, "I am not sending you on any

dangerous mission this time, so you can relax." He continued: "The time for your investiture ceremony is close, so I am taking you both off operations until it is over. As of now, you are officially on leave."

"Thank you, sir. That's fine by us," they replied.

"Good. Then I assume that you will be staying at the Strand Palace Hotel."

"Yes, sir," replied Charlie. "We'll be having a party, and it would be nice if you and your wife could come up to join us."

"That's good of you," said the CO. "I'll try my best to get away. There are some rumblings about us being posted to the Med, but keep it under your hat."

"Will do," replied Charlie. "At least it will be warmer."

"You would think so," said the CO, "in more ways than one!"

Tom rang Caroline to tell her what time he would be arriving.

"I'm taking some leave," he said.

"Oh, darling, that will be fabulous! I'll arrange some time off."

"I'd love to meet your parents."

"That will be good. I never mentioned my dad was in the navy in the last war."

"Blimey!" said Tom. "We should get on really well. Why don't you ask them if they would like to come to the palace?"

"Oh, Tom, are you sure? They would be thrilled – especially Dad. He's asked me several times about you."

"That's settled, then," said Tom. "What was your dad?"

"I think he was a petty officer of some sort. I know he was at the Battle of Jutland."

"Bloody Hell!" said Tom. "We should find plenty to talk about."

"Yes, I think you will. He never talks about it to us – that's usually the way. Probably only those who have been there can really understand what it must be like."

The operator said, "Sorry, sir – your time is up."

"OK," Tom replied. "See you soon, my sweet. Love you."

"Love you too."

The phone went dead.

"Everything all right?" asked Charlie.

"Fine!" replied Tom, and he told him about Caroline's father.

"Well, I never! I hope he enjoys the palace."

"It will be nice to meet him; we will be able to have a good old natter," said Tom.

"It will. My old man was never in the forces, but he is doing his bit now – air-raid warden. He is dead proud when he gets his tin hat on. Mum says she is glad he has found something to do, and she is dead proud as well.

Tom said, "I often think about my folks."

"I know," Charlie replied. "It's a pity you have no brothers or sisters, but you know my folks like to think of you as one of theirs, don't you?"

"Yes," Tom answered, "and I appreciate that, but it's not the same, is it, mate? I would love to get my hands on the bastards who killed them. I would swing for them." (Tom's parents had been killed by a hit-and-run driver who had never been caught.)

"I know, mate, but you have handled it well. That's the kind of guy you are – you seem to make everything look easy."

"Thanks," Tom said, "but having a friend like you makes it a lot more bearable."

"Well, that's enough of being sad," Charlie said. "We have a lot of good things to look forward to now, so let's get on with living."

"Agreed!"

"We had better start getting ready for the big day."

"Don't forget we have to go for our new uniforms tomorrow."

"No, I've not forgotten that."

"Will Nat be coming with us?" Tom asked.

"Oh yes. She will tell us if they are OK or not," said Charlie.

The next day they went to the tailor's to try on their new uniforms, and they got Natalie's approval.

"My word," she exclaimed, "you both look splendid – new rings and all! I will have to keep a eye on you, Lieutenant Higson, or some loose woman will be running off with you."

"Not a chance in hell!" he replied. "If I ever look at another girl, you have my permission to shoot me."

"Oh, I don't mind you looking as long as you don't touch, my love," she said. With that, she gave him a big kiss.

"Hey, come on, you two lovebirds – we still have lots to do," Tom said. "Let's go change back into our other gear; then we can get on."

"There he goes," said Charlie. "He can't help being the skipper." And he laughed.

Tom looked at him and Natalie and said, "OK, then, here is another order. Let's go and have a good lunch and some champagne."

"Aye aye, captain," they both replied, and they saluted.

"But on one condition: I foot the bill."

"Oh no," Natalie interrupted, "only if you let me buy the champagne."

"Consider that request accepted by your commanding officer," Tom replied, laughing.

As they left the shop in fine spirits, the tailor looked at his assistant and said, "It's a pleasure to serve customers like that."

"I wholeheartedly agree, sir," said his assistant.

CHAPTER XIII

The Investiture

They left the base with cheers ringing in their ears.

"What a send-off!" said Natalie.

"It certainly was something," Tom answered. "I felt quite proud, like a real hero."

Charlie said, "It made me feel quite special too."

"You are very special to me, my love," said Natalie.

"That will do for me, darling. As long as I am, that's all that counts," replied Charlie.

A car had been laid on to take them to the station. When they arrived there, the marine driver jumped out and opened the doors; he then stood aside and saluted smartly. Tom returned the salute and thanked him. The car drew away and they walked on to the platform. The London train drew into the station on time, and they got into their first-class compartment. As it left the platform, Charlie produced a bottle of champagne from his case.

"Where did that come from?" Natalie asked.

"From the Royals," replied Charlie.

On it was a card saying, 'All the very best to a pair of real gentlemen, from the Royal Marines of the Harwich base'.

"Oh, now, that's what I call a smashing compliment," Natalie said.

"Well," said Tom, "we had better not waste it, had we?"

With that, Charlie opened it.

"What are we going to drink it out of?" asked Tom.

Charlie produced three glasses from his case, all nicely wrapped up.

"They're not quite the right kind," he said, "but they will do just the same."

Then he poured the champagne into them.

Holding up his glass, Tom said, "A toast to the Royals, and long may they look after us."

"We will drink to that," Natalie and Charlie replied; and they emptied their glasses.

"We can't let the rest go flat, so we might as well finish it off," said Tom.

So they did just that. The three of them shook hands, Natalie gave them both a kiss, and then they settled down for the rest of the journey. They arrived about two hours later. It was quite cold with a wind blowing from the north.

"Come on," said Natalie, "let's go to the buffet and get a nice hot drink. I will pay," she said, "and you two can buy the champagne."

"Typical woman's trick!" Charlie said, laughing.

"Lady's privilege!" she replied.

Tom laughed at them both. "I will say this much: life is never dull with you two around."

They got off the crowded train and Tom spotted Caroline in the crowd at the barrier.

"Grab these," he said, thrusting his bags at Charlie; and then he ran down the platform to her.

They ran into each others arms.

"Oh, Tom, it's so wonderful to see you. I have missed you so much," she cried.

As they embraced and kissed, their friends came up carrying Tom's bags. Caroline embraced them.

"It's so good to be together again," she said.

Natalie held her close and said, "You are always in our thoughts, darling. It is much more difficult for you and Tom than it is for us: we are not separated as much as you are."

"Oh, I don't envy you, Natalie. It must be very hard for you too, knowing how dangerous some of the things they have to do are. You must wonder what state they will come back in."

"It is hard sometimes, but at least I can be there for them when they do come back."

They all made their way to the buffet.

While the tea was being brought out, Caroline whispered as

she snuggled up to Tom, "I am going to take you to bed and not let you leave the bedroom until it is time to go to the palace."

He kissed her and said, "I can't wait."

After drinking their tea they felt a bit warmer; then they got a taxi to the hotel.

The manager and his assistant were in the lobby to greet them, and the rest of the staff were lined up. Some of the guests were looking on and wondering what it was all about. They soon found out, when a banner was unfurled by Phyllis. It read:

Welcome to two young heroes, Lieutenant Charles Higson, DSO, and Lieutenant Thomas Weston, VC.

Everyone joined in the applause.

Natalie turned to Caroline and exclaimed, "What a marvellous welcome!"

Tom walked across to Phyllis and took her arm and said, "Thank you." He gave her a big kiss and a tear came into her eyes.

She looked at them and said, "Thank you to you all. You have changed my whole life completely and brought me so much happiness. If only John could be here, it would complete the day."

"John is coming up," Tom replied. "He wanted to surprise you, so don't tell him I told you. He will be here in the morning."

With that she burst into tears.

"Oh, love, I feel so happy now," she said; and, with that, Tom took her over to the rest of the group.

They all gave her a big hug.

Charlie said, "This is going to be one hell of a party."

Natalie whispered to him, "When I get you upstairs our party will begin."

He took her by the hand and said, "We'd better make it quick; otherwise I will make love to you in the lift."

"Oh, how very kinky!" she said. "I've never done it in a lift before. It could be fun."

"I think you are a scarlet woman," he said with a laugh.

They went up to their room and the manager unlocked the door.

"Welcome! We will try to make this visit something for you to remember for the rest of your lives."

On the table was set out a beautiful array of food and drink, including bottles of wines and champagne.

"Look at it," Tom said. "Isn't that splendid!"

"I think I am having a dream!" Charlie exclaimed.

As long as I am in it with you, I don't mind," replied Natalie.

"Well, as long as I am head waitress I suppose I had better do the honours," Phyllis interjected.

"Oh, no, you won't," said Tom. "You are a special guest, and therefore will be treated as such. Sit down and enjoy yourself."

"Better do has the skipper tells you, Phyllis," Charlie said, "or you will be put on a fizzer."

"What's a fizzer?" asked Phyllis.

"Oh, you don't want to know that," he said: "it could be very painful."

"It sounds a bit scary," laughed Caroline. "I think you had better do as you are told."

They all had a good laugh and got stuck into the food and drink.

Much later, as Tom and Caroline lay in each other's arms he could feel her soft breasts against him.

She said, "You are the best thing that has ever happened to me, darling."

Tom pulled her closer to him. "You know, next Wednesday I will be twenty-one, and in my short life I have seen things that people should never have to see, but meeting you has made them easier to face because your love helps to keep me on an even keel. I seem to be able to look at things in a different light, and you have given me something to live for. Before I met you I was a bit devil-may-care, but now I have grown up."

"My darling Tom, I do worry about you. I get very scared," she said.

"You mustn't worry too much, my sweet. I promise you I am much more careful now."

"Good," she replied. "Now you can make wild passionate love to me again."

They made love passionately and noisily and with complete abandonment as if they hadn't a care in the world.

When they awoke it was dark.

Tom looked at his watch. "It's 7.30," he said.

"Well, does it matter? We can have a quick dinner, and then come back to bed."

Tom pinched her bottom and said, "You are becoming a wicked girl."

"I know," she replied with a giggle. "I feel wicked when I am with you."

"Good. Don't ever change, because I love you just the way you are."

"Well, I suppose we will have to make a move. I have asked Mum and Dad to meet us in the bar at 8.30."

With that, she got out of bed.

"You are the most gorgeous girl I have ever seen in my life."

"I bet you say that to all the girls, don't you?" She gave him a cheeky wink.

He gave her a look and said, "There will never be any other girls for me. Race you to the bathroom."

Forty-five minutes later they walked into the bar.

"There they are," Caroline said, pointing her father and mother out to Tom.

"I can see where you get your good looks from: your mum is lovely, and your dad is a rather handsome man."

As they reached the table, her father stood up and took Tom's hand.

"It's so good to meet you at last," he said, shaking Tom's hand.

Tom kissed Caroline's mother on her cheek and said, "It is a pleasure to meet you both."

"Caroline has told me so much about you that I feel I know you already," her father replied. "I am so proud that she has found a decent man at last – and one who is in the Andrew."

"Thank you," Tom replied. "I promise you both I will never let her down."

"What's the Andrew?" asked Caroline.

"The Royal Navy," her father replied. "That's what sailors call it."

"Oh, I see. I didn't know that," she replied.

"Right, what will it be?" her father asked.

"Well, I fancy a large horse's neck," Tom said. "What would you like?" he asked Caroline and her mother.

"What's a horse's neck?" Caroline asked.

"It's a brandy bitters," her father said.

"Well, I will try one of those, then."

Tom and her father looked at each other and grinned.

"OK, that's what we will all have," her father said. He called over the waiter to order.

When the drinks arrived, Caroline's father proposed a toast: "To a happy and long and successful life to you both."

"We will drink to that."

As they took a drink, Tom saw Caroline grimace. He looked at her father and they both gave a little smile. She said nothing, but she finished it off and put her glass down.

"I am proud of you, darling," Tom said. "You are very brave."

Her father said to Tom, "We must swap stories some time about the Andrew."

"Yes, that will be interesting," he replied.

"That will be something to listen to!" Caroline's mother exclaimed. "He never talks to us about what he did in the war."

"Well, you wouldn't understand if I told you."

"Maybe not, but it would be nice to hear your stories. Oh, by the way, I am Helen and this is Stuart as no one has introduced us, Tom."

"Oh," he answered, "I'm sure we would have got around to it sooner or later."

Charlie and Natalie arrived in the bar and came across to join them. Tom stood up and said, "This is my very best mate, Lieutenant Charles Higson – Charlie to his friends – and this is the very lovely Natalie James, 1st officer in the Wrens, without whom our base would come to a standstill." Then he introduced Helen and Stuart.

After handshakes, Charlie asked, "What are you all drinking?"

Caroline said, "Not horse's necks, that is for sure!" and everyone laughed.

"Well, what's the big joke?" asked Natalie.

"Well, I tried one earlier and it was awful," said Caroline. "Tom and my dad thought it was a great laugh. But don't you worry, Lieutenant Weston, I will get my own back."

Helen asked, "Have you and Tom known each other a long time, then, Charlie?"

"We went to school together – first infants, then juniors, then secondary school, and then naval college. In 1937 we both passed out as sub lieutenants and volunteered for the small-boat section. So yes, you could say we have known each other all our lives."

"I think that is absolutely marvellous," Helen replied.

Natalie and Caroline looked at each other and burst into tears.

"What on earth is the matter?" asked Tom.

"We think that is the most beautiful story we have ever heard," they replied.

"Here," Charlie said, passing his large handkerchief over, "dry your eyes and let's have a drink."

After that, the evening went really well.

They put Caroline's parents in a taxi at the end of the evening and Tom said, "Will we see you again before the big day?"

"Yes, we hope so."

With that, the taxi pulled away and they went home.

The big day arrived at last. All of them were up early. Caroline phoned her parents to make sure they were up.

"Everything OK at home?" asked Tom.

"Yes, they are up and raring to go."

They all had a good breakfast and then started to prepare for the ceremony.

Charlie said, "I am more nervous now than if I was going on a mission."

"Me too," replied Tom, "but it isn't every day that you get to meet the King of England, is it?"

They all showered. Then the two girls went into one bedroom to get themselves ready, while the boys went into the other.

"Well, do you think we will do?" Natalie said about forty minutes later.

"I hope so," replied Caroline. "It's too late now to change."

They went into the lounge to wait. A few minutes later the boys emerged.

"You both look absolutely wonderful," they said. They stood there resplendent in their new uniforms.

"Will we do, then?" they asked.

"You are going to turn everyone's heads today."

"As long as we turn your heads that will do," replied Tom.

There was a knock on the door.

"I'll get it," said Natalie.

She opened the door and Caroline's parents came in.

"You were quick."

"Quick?" said her father. "Helen has been ready since first light."

"Well, you both do us credit," Charlie told them.

"Would you like a coffee or a tea?"

"I wouldn't mind something stronger if you have anything," Stuart said.

"No, you don't!" Helen told him.

"Oh well – coffee, then, I suppose. You all look really smart." Helen continued: "You look like models out of a magazine."

"Well, thank you. That's a nice compliment," Natalie said.

Stuart said, "I feel more nervous now than I felt before Jutland."

"That's something you can tell us about over a few pints one day," said Tom.

"I don't get out much these days – only to the Legion at the weekends," Stuart replied.

Tom said, "That sounds fine by me. Consider it a date."

Charlie suddenly let out a cry.

"What the hell's up with you?" Natalie asked.

"What's up? I've got to meet Mum and Dad's train at King's Cross and it's due in fifteen minutes."

"Why didn't you say, you silly ass?" Natalie responded.

Stuart said, "I could go and meet them for you. Have you a photo of them? I'll take them to the palace from there."

"Oh, could you? That would be a great help." He took a photograph from his wallet and gave it to Stuart.

Tom was on the phone ordering a taxi. "It will be here in five minutes," he said.

Stuart left to go the station.

"If it's on time, they could be there before us," Natalie said, looking at Charlie. "You would lose your head if it was loose."

"It is loose. It only thinks of you, though," he said, grinning.

"Oh, come on, then – I love you just as much, loose or not."

Caroline came out of the bathroom.

"Where is Dad?" she asked.

Charlie explained what had happened and apologised.

"Oh, that's OK. These things happen, and we have all been a bit uptight."

Tom looked across. "A right bloody pair we are! It's a good job we've got these two."

"I know," Charlie replied, "but I think it will be OK by my parents. I will apologise when I see them."

The phone rang and Natalie picked it up.

"Thank you," she said. "Cars are here," she announced.

"There, you see – the girls are doing all the hard work for us, and we are like a couple of bloody jellyfish."

"Ah, but they aren't the ones that have to stand in front of the King."

"Point taken, Lieutenant Higson."

"Thank you, Lieutenant Weston, sir." He saluted and they shook hands. "It's a big day for us both, mate."

And so off they went.

Tom looked at his watch. "Well, sweetheart," he said, "I am as ready as I ever will be." He took her hand. "Let's go."

"You look tremendous, darling, and I feel so proud of you. I love you," Caroline replied, and she gave him a kiss.

"What time is Phyllis getting here?" he asked.

"She may be here now; she should be in Reception."

"John phoned last night to tell her he would meet her at the hotel. I left their passes at the desk for them."

They all went down in the lift. When they walked into the hall, Phyllis and John met them.

John took his skipper's hand. "Well done!" he said. "It couldn't have happened to a nicer bloke. All the crew send their best wishes."

Phyllis gave Tom a hug and Caroline a kiss. She said, "I haven't known you very long, Tom, but I am so pleased to have met you. I think you are a good man." She looked at her friend. "You are a very lucky girl. God has been very good to you."

Helen asked, "Are your parents coming, Natalie?"

"No, my mother died two years ago, and my father is in the Med at the moment. He's an admiral out there, so I don't see much of him."

"Oh, I am sorry."

"That's OK," she answered.

"Is everyone ready? The cars will be waiting."

"Are we going by taxi?" asked Helen.

"No. Cars have been laid on by the hotel," Tom told her.

The crowds at the palace were tremendous. It took them a while to get through the gates.

"Bloody hell!" Charlie cried. "I've never seen so many people in my life."

"That's because they've come to see you and Tom receive your medals," said Natalie.

"Don't be silly," he replied. "There are bloody dozens of us getting them."

The cars finally drew up at the entrance and they all alighted. Charlie's parents and Caroline's father were waiting to greet them. Caroline took Tom's arm.

He looked at her. "You look better than any film star. You will make everyone very jealous, darling," he added. "And, Natalie, I haven't seen you in a dress before. You look absolutely bloody marvellous."

"She is, mate," Charlie retorted, "and she is all mine."

John and Phyllis looked on.

"Don't they look a stunning sight?" she said.

John squeezed her hand, looked at her and replied, "You are better than all the medals in the world."

As he looked at Phyllis, Charlie said to Tom, "If she isn't the most striking girl on this planet, I will eat my hat. Sorry, Nat, my love, but that's just the way I feel."

"Don't be sorry," she replied. "I think most folks would agree with you."

They were ushered into a large antechamber by one of the King's equerries. When all the medal recipients were assembled, a major general in the guards came into the room. He explained everything that would take place and carried on to say, "As there is only one receiver of the Victoria Cross" – and he looked across at Tom as he said it – "Lieutenant Weston will be the last to receive his medal."

"Bloody hell!" Tom whispered to Charlie. "What do I say to the King if he asks me anything?"

"Ask him how his missus is," Charlie replied with a grin.

"You are a fat lot of help, mate."

"Well, I don't bloody know – I am too scared about what I will say if he talks to me."

"It's more bloody scary than most of the ops we've ever done."

While the relatives and friends were waiting to go into the main chamber, Natalie spotted Tom's coxswain and some of his crew in the crowd.

She nudged Caroline. "There are some of the crews, and it looks like wives and girlfriends, over there," she said. She went over to a captain of the guards who was standing there. "Excuse me," she said, putting on her best smile.

"Yes, madam? Is there anything I can do for you?"

She explained about Tom receiving his medal and pointed out the coxswain and the others with him. "Would there be any possible chance of getting them in to see him receive it?"

He said, "I won't promise you anything, madam, but I will see what can be done."

She thanked him and gave him a peck on the cheek. As she walked away he gave her a salute and said, "I think you have just sealed a bargain, Miss."

When she returned to the others, Caroline asked her what he had said.

"I think there is every chance that the crews may see the boys get their medals."

"That will be fabulous. What a lovely surprise!"

With that, two large doors were flung open and they were invited to go inside. A servant resplendent in the royal livery showed them into what could be described as the most sumptuous and lavishly furnished room any of them had ever seen. At the far end was a small raised dais. On it where two huge thrones, and on either side stood a guardsman in full dress uniform.

Charlie's father said to his wife, "To think our two boys are going to get a medal from His Majesty in here! It is like a fairy tale come true."

"I feel so proud of them both," she answered.

Suddenly another door opened at the side of the small dais. Two guardsmen came smartly to attention and presented arms. After a small pause, the King and Queen came into the room side by side, looking wonderful. His Majesty escorted the Queen to her throne and she sat down; then he sat on his throne. A fanfare was blown and the proceedings began. A hush fell over the room. The King came forward to stand at the front of the dais.

As each medal recipient came forward to receive his or her award, an officer of the guards brought the decoration on a small velvet cushion. A citation was read out and the medal pinned to the chest of the person who received it. This went on for some time.

At last Charlie stepped up to receive his DSO. He stood smartly to attention as His Majesty pinned it to his chest. The King had a short conversation with him, and Charlie saluted, turned about and marched over to where Natalie was waiting. She took his hand and he kissed her as the families smiled and looked on. The ceremony carried on for about another thirty minutes. The King returned to his throne and sat down.

After quite a time had passed, the audience relaxed a little and there was another fanfare. The King arose and came forward to the edge of the dais. Tom, accompanied by a major general carrying a maroon velvet cushion, approached the dais and halted. Another officer followed them, and when he reached the dais he turned to face the audience, unrolled a parchment and began to speak:

"Ladies and gentlemen," he began. "The last presentation to be given by His Majesty King George the Sixth, King of England and Emperor of India and the Dominions, will be to Lieutenant Thomas Weston of His Majesty's Royal Navy Small Boat section, for gallantry above and beyond the call of duty. He did, in the face of the enemy, not thinking of his own safety, though seriously wounded himself, take his own boat alongside a burning and sinking boat of his own flotilla to effect the rescue of every crewman on board. For this action Lieutenant Thomas Weston, DSC, will receive the highest honour for bravery in the land – the Victoria Cross – from His Royal Majesty King George the Sixth."

Tom stepped forward and stood smartly to attention in front of the King. The King took the award from the velvet cushion and pinned the medal to his chest. He stooped a little and spoke to him:

"Lieutenant Weston, the Queen and I, and the whole country, salute you for your bravery. With men like yourself and these other brave men, we cannot fail to prevail in this awful conflict."

He shook Tom's hand and Tom replied, "Thank you, Your Majesty."

He stepped back from the dais, saluted, about-turned and marched over to where his friends and their families were standing. There were tears streaming down Caroline's face. He took her by the hand, took out his handkerchief and dabbed her tears. Then he kissed her on both cheeks. The whole room burst into applause.

Caroline had never felt so proud of anyone before. She whispered, "I love you, Tom, with all my heart, and I promise I will never do anything to make you ashamed of me."

After the investiture Tom faced a barrage of cameras and reporters all shouting questions at him, but he insisted that Charlie be in the photographs with him. After quite a time they managed to get to their cars and drove back to the hotel, where the party was in full swing.

Tom, to his complete surprise and delight, discovered that his coxswain and some of his and Charlie's crews had returned ahead of them from the palace so they could all continue the festivities together.

Helen asked Charlie's mother, "There is one thing puzzling me – I hope you don't mind me asking? – why is it that Tom never talks about his parents?"

Charlie's mother replied that Tom's parents had both been killed in a hit-and-run accident.

"Oh, my goodness!" Helen exclaimed. "How awful! The poor boy!"

"We try to treat him like one of ours and it has seemed to help him. It looks like he may be your son-in-law soon."

"I do hope so," Helen replied. "They do make a lovely couple."

Caroline came over. "Everything all right?" she asked. "You seem to be looking very serious about something."

Helen explained: "Charlie's mother was saying I might have a new son-in-law soon."

"Maybe one day when everything is sorted out. We will have to tell his parents soon."

Her mother gasped. "Oh, you don't know!" she said.

"Know what?" asked Caroline. "Have I said something wrong?"

"Tom hasn't any family," Helen said.

"He never talks about them. What do you mean?"

"His parents are both dead. They were killed in a road accident."

"Oh!" she cried out. "My poor love!"

Tom saw her run into the bedroom in tears, and he went after her. She was sitting on the bed crying her heart out.

"What on earth is the matter, darling?" he asked her. "You were so happy just now. Why this? It's not anything I have done, is it?"

She put her arms around him. "Oh, darling, I didn't know about your parents."

Tom held her close to him. He said to her, "I know I should have told you, sweet. I try not to talk about them, but they would have been so proud to meet you, I know." Tom explained what had happened and told her that the person driving the other car had never been caught.

"Oh, my sweetheart," she replied, "you must have been devastated. Do you miss them a lot? You must do."

"Yes, I do," he confessed. "I often think about them and what it would be like if they were here now."

"They would have been so proud of you today, as we all are. I know I can't alter what has happened, but I'm sure they are always with you. I know that your work is dangerous, but I try to be strong for you."

74

He held her tightly and kissed her. "I know how lucky I am to have you, so let's go and enjoy life to the full."

After the party and a couple of days' rest, Tom and Caroline decided to go to the countryside for some peace and quiet. They wanted to be alone together.

"We will go to the Lake District, and on the way we can call on Charlie and his parents," Tom said.

"Oh yes," Caroline replied. "I want to share everything with you for the rest of our lives. It will be wonderful to be just the two of us to do anything we please."

"I think Charlie's mum knows someone who rents out a small cottage up there."

"That will be fabulous, darling. We can go for country walks and then make love all night."

"I don't know about the walks, but I like the idea of the love-making," he replied.

"You are a sex maniac," she said.

"Well, that makes two of us, then."

"Oh, by the way, what with the investiture and all the other things that have happened, I forget to tell you about my divorce."

"Well, come on – tell me now. I can't wait to hear."

"Well, the solicitors seem to think they can finalise it by the end of next month."

"That's great news!" he cried. "We will get engaged and take it from there. It will mean you are really mine for ever then."

They spent the rest of their time together doing what they said they would do. Then, when Tom's leave was over, they returned to London and he went back to the war.

CHAPTER XIV

Felixstowe

Tom had been out on another mission and was returning to base yet again.

"I wonder how many more bloody jaunts we will do before this bleeding war is over?"

They had been on duty for two weeks, and they had already completed eight missions.

"I could do with a bloody good rest," Charlie said.

"Me too," was Tom's reply. "Anyway, let's go out tonight and get bloody drunk."

"Great idea, mate. Natalie is up at her aunt's place – someone's ill, I think."

"OK, that's settled, then. I'll try to give Caroline a ring, and then we'll do the town."

The two friends got ready and went on a bender. The next morning they were woken up by a knock on the door.

"Who the hell is it?" Charlie yelled. "Come on in – it's not bloody locked. What time is it?" he asked. "Oh, my poor bloody head!"

Tom looked at his watch. "It's 6.30," he replied.

A seaman came in.

"The CO would like to see you both in his office, sir – as soon as possible."

"OK. Tell him we are on our way."

"Right, sir – will do."

The seaman turned and left, muttering to himself, "Bloody officers! They think they own the whole friggin' world."

"Come on – let's see what he wants."

"It must be bloody urgent for him to call us at this time of day," Charlie said.

"Well, let's go and find out."

They both dressed in a hurry, had a quick wash and left the room.

"Not a bad morning," said Charlie. "It could turn out to be a nice day."

Arriving at the office, they knocked on the door and a voice said, "Come in."

On entering, they saw Natalie sitting there behind her desk.

"When did you get back?" they both asked.

"Oh, late last night," she replied.

"What's it all about? Any idea?"

"None at all," she said. "Go straight in."

"It's nice to have you back, love," said Charlie, and then he gave her quick kiss.

The CO looked up. "Ah, there you are! I've got a job for you both. Sit down and I will tell you about it."

They gave each other a quick glance and sat down.

"We are all ears, sir."

The CO began: "We need two boats for a raiding party."

"Where?" asked Tom.

"You will be told that when you get to the pickup point."

"Where is that, sir?"

"Felixstowe."

"Isn't that a fishing port, sir?" asked Charlie. "That seems a strange place for a pickup."

"Well, that's where they want you," was the reply. "They want two experienced crews; that's why the job's yours."

"When do we leave, sir?"

"At 1300 hours. You will be given the rest of the brief when you arrive. That's as much as I am authorised to tell you at this point."

"Right, sir. We'd better round up the boys and get the boats ready. Have we time to eat, sir?"

"Of course. You can't go to war on an empty stomach."

As they left the office, Charlie asked Natalie if everything was OK at home.

She replied, "Yes, but my sister was ill."

"I didn't know you had a sister."

"You wouldn't like her if you met her. She's rather too stuck-up for my liking. I don't know why."

"Ah well! I won't miss much, then, by not meeting her."

"What's the op?" Natalie asked.

"We're just escorting a raiding party of commandos. We don't know much else."

She came round her desk and put her arms around him.

"Just you be careful, Charlie Higson. I want you back in one piece."

"I will, darling," he replied, and he gave her a big kiss.

A couple of hours later, Tom and Charlie were stood in front of their crews, giving them a short briefing on the op.

"We want the boats in top order," Tom said.

"Are we carrying torpedoes, sir?"

"I'm not sure if they are required, but we can take them along. If we don't need them, we can offload them at Felixstowe."

The day was bright with a slight wind, which was causing a slow swell.

"Warmin' up nicely," Charlie remarked, "and clear skies, mate. We'd better keep an eye out for aircraft."

"Aye, we don't want them to surprise us by coming out of the sun. We'd better test the guns as soon as we clear the harbour."

"Good idea, and let's keep a fair distance between us. We don't want to make it too easy for them if they are about."

Later on, in the chart room Tom was pondering over the charts with his navigator.

"The minefields are pretty well inshore," John said, "but the current can be fairly strong in some places where the rivers come out into the sea."

"Ever been to Felixstowe?" Tom asked John.

"Can't say I have," he replied. "I know it's a fishing port, so we can expect plenty of traffic in and out."

"We'd best keep our eyes out for some hefty trawlers, then – most likely the deep-sea kind."

78

"Yes, we don't want to bump into one of them. The weather reports are good – plenty of clear sky and the wind freshening from the north. We could get some quite rough seas with that forecast.

"Let me know if anything comes through on the set," said Tom as he left the chart room.

"Aye aye, sir."

On the bridge the lookouts had their glasses up, keeping a good lookout in case of trouble.

The coxswain, on the wheel, asked, "Everything OK, sir?"

"It is. Course 220. Let's keep this speed up as long as we can. It looks like we will get some rougher seas later."

The coxswain looked at the gyrocompass and replied, "Right, sir. I think it's time for a brew, skipper," said he. He asked one of the lookouts to organise it, adding, "I will keep your station while you do it."

"Aye aye, sir."

"Oh, and put a tot in it. I think we may need it later."

A steady course was kept. Though there was quite a swell running, 326 went through it nice and smoothly. They were cruising at 18 knots.

The brew arrived on the bridge.

"The crew have had theirs, sir."

"Good. I'm off to the wardroom. If there are any problems, call me."

The wardroom was quite large for this type of craft. Tom looked around and listened to the throb of the Packard engines. 'Very reassuring!' he thought. He sat down and wondered what Caroline was doing. He thought, 'It's good to have someone to think about. It keeps me from feeling alone – even at sea.'

It took them another few hours to reach Felixstowe. When they arrived there was a hell of a lot of ships about, just as John had predicted. The harbour was absolutely chocka with trawlers of every size. Most were loading, ready to put out to sea; a few were unloading their catches.

The MTBs were met by a small pilot to guide them to their berth. It had been an uneventful trip, except for the sea roughening up. After berthing, Tom and Charlie were met by a major.

"Well, I never! It's bloody Tom Weston."

The major was Graham Yates, whom Tom had met whilst he was recovering after his injury the year before.

"I never expected to see you," Tom said.

"Nor me you," Graham replied as he shook Tom and Charlie by the hand. "You are sight for sore eyes. It's good to have you with us."

John came down and shook hands with the Major too.

"So, are you in charge of this show, then?" Tom asked him.

"No such luck! I'm the number two. Colonel Mark Shaunessy is the boss. Come along and meet him. He's a good man."

CHAPTER XV

The Raid

Colonel Shaunessy was a big man – six foot two inches, at least, and around fourteen stone – and he was as fit as a fiddle. He shook hands with Tom and Charlie.

"Good trip?" he asked.

"It was," they replied.

"Glad to have you with us. I've heard a lot about you both," he said.

"All good, I hope!" said Charlie.

"Well, most of it," the Colonel replied with a grin. "I believe you already know Graham."

"We certainly do."

"Good – that makes the job easier. Come into the office and I will give you the details of the mission. Please take a seat."

They both pulled up chairs and sat opposite the Colonel.

"Sergeant, please organise some refreshments for our guests."

"Will do, sir," said the Sergeant.

"And put a drop of the good stuff in it. We have three days to put this raid together. My lads have been rehearsing for a couple of weeks, so all that is needed is to get your part organised. The raid is on a radar station on the coast of Belgium. It is in a position where the bombers can't get an accurate drop, and it is well guarded. If we can surprise them, we should be able to pull it off and blow the whole bloody thing sky high."

The refreshments arrived.

"Blimey!" Charlie exclaimed. "He's a big lad."

"He is. We used to play rugby together before this lot happened."

"Really? Who did you play for?"

"Munster. Those were the days, until Herr Hitler decided to have some fun! Anyway, back down to business: there will be sixty officers and men, mostly guards, involved with this op. They will be transported by two armed trawlers specially fitted out for the job. Your job is to escort us across the Channel and, frankly, to cover our arses. It's got to be a smallish force so as not to attract too much attention."

"Sounds straightforward enough," said Tom.

Colonel Shaunessy continued: "So when we go in, it will be up to you to deal with any E-boats or other enemy vessels that might come nosing around. We have information from the Resistance that there are no E-boats close, but there are a couple of old gunboats and a small lightly armed destroyer somewhere about. The garrison is about thirty strong, but it is about five miles away. The trawlers will take us in to a small jetty and unload us there. When we arrive, it will be your job to patrol the coast and deal with any odd Jerries that might wander on to the scene. If the raid is successful, you need to be ready to take us off and get us away as quick as possible. If it goes wrong, we may have to signal you; but that will be discussed fully in the main briefing on the day of the op."

The next two days were spent rehearsing. They practised in a small cove with similar currents and eddies to the cove near the radar station in Belgium.

The main briefing was held at 1100 hours on the day of the raid. After the briefing, a meal was provided, and everyone took a good rest. The night was as black as the inside of a bag. The weather had worsened considerably, with a strong wind from the north. As they boarded their boats, Tom and Charlie wished each other good luck. They had a final word with Colonel Shaunessy and Graham and then shook hands. The op was now on.

The coxswain was on the bridge awaiting orders. Tom was in the chart room with John.

"It looks like being a rough night," John said. " The sea is going to be bloody rough with the wind this strong and coming from the north."

It was 2200 hours when they left the quay.

Todd said to his mate on the Bofors gun, "I think it'll be time for a good piss-up after this."

"No difference there, then!" Les replied.

"Are you insinuating I'm a boozer?"

"Would I do anything like that, mate!" replied Todd, and they both had a good laugh.

The engines assumed a nice throaty throb. The engine room was just in front of the stokers' and seamen's mess, next to the fuel tanks holding 30,000 gallons of high-octane fuel. Yorkie listened to the twin Packards with satisfaction.

"They sound good and tight," he said to his friend. "Let's hope they stay that way and some bloody stray bullet don't hit the bleeding tanks."

"Well, if it does, we won't know much about it, will we?"

"Bloody cheerful, you are," his mate retorted. "We may get some leave after this mission."

"Good. I will spend the whole time in bed with the missus." (Reg hadn't been married very long. His wife was only twenty.)

"You're a lucky bleeder," Yorkie replied.

"Well, don't you miss your missus?"

"Nah – I think she's having it off with the bleeding butcher."

Tom was back on the bridge.

"It's bloody dark," he said, looking at the gyrocompass. "Keep her steady, Dave. We don't want to lose them in this dark. We would have a hell of job finding them again. Keep a good lookout, lads."

They all had night glasses, but it wasn't easy with the strong spray coming over the bridge screen like bullets, and they had to be constantly wiped to keep them clear.

On 324, Charlie was looking at the nearest trawler. It was pitching badly, and he pitied the troops on it.

"There will be a few throwing up on that boat," he said.

"I wouldn't fancy being in it myself," replied his number one.

"Well, keep an eye on her, Neil."

"Aye aye, skip."

"I'm off to the chart room," said Charlie.

On 326, the tension was building as the weather grew worse. They had to concentrate more and more. Tom could see the trawler having a rough time of it, but even so they were making a good 20 knots. They were still on schedule, but it had started to rain heavily.

"Bit wet now," said the coxswain, pulling on his waterproofs.

"Aye, but it's good cover, and they won't be expecting a raid in this weather," Tom answered. "Keep your eyes open all the same, though."

The coast of Belgium was getting nearer all the time, and the tension was mounting. Everyone was fully alert to the possible dangers. When the shoreline came into view, it was time to cock and load all the guns.

"It looks as though we are going to be lucky and catch Jerry with his bloody pants down."

"Looks that way, sir," one of the gunners said.

"Watch for that signal – we don't want to miss it."

The trawlers were going in to land the troops.

"This is it, lads," shouted Tom. One of the lookouts yelled, "The commandos are going in. I can see them jumping ashore, sir."

Firing started as they started to move inland.

"There must be a pillbox there, sir," someone shouted.

"The commandos will deal with that."

Tom heard the Browning click. He looked behind and saw the Bofors gun swinging out. 'Well,' he thought, 'the lads are alert.'

The trawlers at the quayside opened fire again as the commandos moved further inland.

Tom yelled, "Keep a bloody eye open for any enemy vessels."

His number one shouted, "Jerry destroyer coming in fast to starboard, sir."

"Open fire when she comes into range."

The enemy ship opened fire first. Being an old ship, her armament wasn't heavy. As it came into range, flares were fired which lit up the sky. The destroyer was firing too high, and, as tracer flew over 326, they opened fire with all guns that could be brought to bear. Tom could see hit after hit on the enemy vessel. She swung away, and the coxswain immediately swung the wheel to follow her course.

As the destroyer turned broadside on, Tom yelled, "Fire torpedoes!"

Both torpedoes were fired, and he could see them heading straight for the destroyer. It didn't stand a chance in hell. The two torpedoes struck her amidships, and the explosion was enormous. The German ship immediately began to list. As they turned away, Tom saw 324 engaging the gunboats. Charlie's boat was scoring hits with everything she had.

Tom yelled, "Take us in to help 324."

Again the coxswain swung the wheel hard over, taking them closer in to engage the enemy gunboats.

The enemy vessels took terrible punishment from the two MTBs. One blew up after taking a hit on what was obviously an ammo box. It disappeared in seconds. The other one turned away, making as much smoke as possible, and was soon lost in the dark.

The MTBs turned their attention towards the shore, and a terrific explosion was seen inland.

"It looks as if the boys have achieved their objective," Tom said.

With that, a cheer went round the boat.

There was a lot of firing, and flares lit up the sky. Tom could see the commandos fighting their way back to the quay. He spotted a flash of light and picked up his night glasses. Focusing in, he saw what looked liked a line of vehicles on a road coming towards the quay.

He shouted, "Jerry convoy, bearing 240 degrees. Open fire, all guns."

Immediately everything they had was brought to bear on the enemy convoy.

"You OK?" Charlie shouted as 324 came alongside.

"Yes," Tom yelled back over the noise.

"There's a hell of a bloody fight going on out there; I wouldn't fancy being in that. Do you have any damage?" he asked.

"A little," was the reply. "I think I've taken one in the shoulder," Tom said, "but I don't thinks it's serious."

There were vehicles burning all along the road by now. The trawlers were moving in to pick up the commandos. The two

MTBs continued to pound the convoy. Suddenly a huge explosion lit up the sky.

"It must've been carrying bloody ammo," someone remarked.

"They wouldn't have felt owt," another voice said.

The commandos had reached the quay and were beginning to get aboard their transport home.

Charlie shouted across, "The trawlers are leaving the quay." A signal went up, telling them to withdraw; they came out fast. The two MTBs followed them out to sea. After clearing the cove, they increased speed to 25 knots and headed for home.

"As long as nothing follows us, we should be OK," said Tom.

"Should be!" his number one replied.

The coxswain on the wheel asked, "Shall we take up stations, sir?"

"Yes, we better had."

Tom saw 324 turning to starboard to take up its position.

A message came from the lead trawler. It said, 'Well done, and thanks for all your help.'

Tom replied, 'It was our pleasure.'

The whole operation had taken just over an hour and a half.

'God, is that all! It seemed a bloody sight longer than that,' Tom said to himself.

He looked at Harry, his number one, and said, "I wonder if Charlie took any damage."

"Sorry, sir, I don't know," was the reply.

"He said he took one in his shoulder."

"Bloody hell! I didn't know that. How are you feeling, sir?"

"A bit sore. John will take a look at it as soon as we are clear," Tom said. "I'm sure young Alan will be looking after Charlie."

"He'll be OK," replied Harry. "Alan was studying to be a doctor before he joined up."

"I didn't know that," Tom said. "It's a good job, though! Natalie would never forgive me if anything happened to Charlie. That girl dotes on him."

"Lucky beggar! I wish I had someone to dote on me."

"Right, we will have to find you someone."

"Thanks all the same, but I think I'll find my own. Let's go home."

They got back to Felixstowe and Tom and Charlie met on the quay. They looked at each other and burst out laughing.

"Bloody hell! Don't we look a right pair of pillocks!" (They both had their left arm in a sling.)

As they walked along, Graham caught them up. "Well done, the pair of you!" he said. "The CO is dead chuffed. You did an excellent job. How are the arms?" he asked.

"Not too bad," they both replied. "Could have been worse."

"It hurts like hell," Charlie replied with a smile. "Young Alan should get a bloody medal for treating the wounded."

"How did your lot fare?"

"We lost six good lads, and I think about a dozen wounded – none of them seriously, thank God."

After a day's rest and doing some minor repairs, they returned to base.

CHAPTER XVI

A Short Break

When the news came through that Charlie had been wounded, Natalie was beside herself.

"Oh no," she cried, "not my darling Charlie!"

Marion, who was with her, said, "I know, love, how you feel, but it only says 'wounded'; it doesn't say 'seriously wounded' or anything."

"I don't think I could go on if anything happens to him."

"I know, but if he is badly hurt, he will need you to be strong," she replied, holding Natalie's hands. "I will try to find out if any more information has come through."

Marion went to the signals room and asked the petty officer in charge if there was any more news.

"I'll have a look for you."

"Thanks," Marion said.

There had been casualties: the commandos had six killed, and six wounded (none seriously) included two officers. In less than two hours they had inflicted heavy losses on the enemy, including massive damage to enemy vessels, and they had completely destroyed the radar station.

Charlie had been taken to hospital, where they removed a bullet and some shrapnel. He also had sustained a broken shoulder and, as a result, had to be kept in. Tom had had a round removed from his arm, but he had been released.

There was only slight damage to 326, but 324 needed major repairs. Charlie asked if he could make a call to the base, but he was told all lines were busy.

"Bloody hell! Natalie will be worried sick, wondering what's happening."

"Don't fret, mate. I will see as her soon as I get back, so you make sure you do as you're bloody well told and get yourself well."

Back at the base, Marion went back to the office.

"Did you find anything out?" asked Natalie.

"Yes, love."

"What is it? Please tell me."

"Charlie has been taken to hospital, and they are keeping him in for observation."

"I knew it! He's badly wounded, isn't he?" Floods of tears streamed down her face. "Oh, Marion, what am I going to do?"

"Now, come on," her friend answered, taking her hand. "Be strong. His boat was damaged; so was he. Young Alan took two bullets out and cleaned the wound. They say Charlie will be able to return with 324 in about four days."

"Oh, thank God he's all right! I'm so glad you were here. When I see him, I'm going to give Alan the biggest hug and kiss he has ever had."

"He must be a wonderful boy; he is only nineteen years old," her friend replied. "He's been recommended for an award."

"That bloody Hitler has a lot to bloody answer for," said Natalie.

"Oh, I am sure he will get his just deserts," Marion said. "Anyway, I'm off – they will think I've deserted if I'm away much longer."

Four days later Tom escorted 324 back to base in case they ran into difficulties. He had waited while she was being patched up.

The sea was running very rough, and they were able to make only 15 knots all the way. As 324 and 326 slid alongside the quay they were greeted with a big cheer by most of the base.

Commander Dolin met the two friends on the quay.

He shook hands and said, "Congratulations are in order. Well done again! Are you OK, Lieutenant Higson?" he asked.

"Yes, sir," Charlie replied. "I'm feeling a bit groggy, but other than that I'm OK. I'm glad to be back at base. The guys I admire are the commandos; they're as hard as bloody nails – and brave.

My God, I'm just pleased they're on our side."

"I'll second that," Tom said.

Natalie ran over to Charlie, flung her arms around his neck and kissed him.

"Where is Alan?" she asked.

"In the wardroom, I think," replied Charlie.

"There's something I have to do," Natalie said, and with that she went on board and made her way down to the wardroom, where Alan was sitting at a small table writing in his log.

He looked up and said, "Hello. Can I help?"

"Yes, you can," replied Natalie. "Come here, you lovely man."

Alan looked at her with complete surprise.

"What have I done? Have I done something wrong?" he asked.

Natalie put her arms around his waist, pulled him towards her and kissed him full on the lips.

"What was that for?" he said, turning crimson.

"For saving the life of the man I love."

With that, she smiled and left the wardroom.

After giving in their reports, Tom and Charlie went to their room to shower and change; 324 and 326 went in for a full overhaul. The two men had further check-ups at the hospital and were given three weeks' sick leave. Tom rang Caroline and told her as much as he was allowed, and they arranged to meet at the hotel. From there they planned to go up to the Lakes, calling in at Charlie's parents for a couple of days on the way.

When Tom arrived at the hotel, Caroline was waiting. She rushed into his arms.

"Oh, darling, I was so worried when Natalie rang and told me what had happened to you."

They kissed while some of the other guests looked on in amazement.

One old lady said, "Well, look at those two – and in public too!"

One of the staff standing close by heard her.

"Madam," he said, "that young man has just been wounded on a very dangerous mission, and he holds the Victoria Cross for defending people like you."

With that, he turned and walked briskly away.

Tom spent four days with Caroline's parents, who kindly slept at the neighbours so they could be alone at night. They all went to the British Legion Club on the second night. As they entered, the trio on stage struck up with 'For He's a Jolly Good Fellow', and Tom noticed the banner above the stage, which read:

WELCOME TO LT TOM WESTON, VC.

A good night was had by all, and quite a lot was drunk. Caroline's father and Tom swapped yarns.

After he left Caroline's parents, Tom went on to Manchester to spend a day or two with Charlie's parents.

"The cottage is all fixed up, so there's nothing for you to do but have a good time up there."

When they arrived, they took a taxi from the station to the cottage.

"How much?" said Tom.

The driver, looking at the purple ribbon on his chest, said, "Nothing, sir. Anyone who holds that doesn't pay me."

"Thank you. That's very kind of you," said Tom. "Will you accept this?" he said, opening his valise and producing a large bottle of rum.

"Why, thank you, sir. I would be honoured. If you need a taxi, give this number a ring any time." He handed a card to Tom and drove off.

The cottage was all prepared.

Caroline looked at him. "Take me to bed," she said. "I love you."

They spent a wonderful week together and then returned to London. After a further couple of days together, Caroline went to the station to see him go back to base.

Tom said, "I have had the most wonderful time. I love you very, very much indeed. So please look after yourself for me."

They embraced and off he went to war again.

CHAPTER XVII

Rendezvous

The two MTBs, 324 and 326, had come back from the repair yard.

Tom said, "Don't they look great – all new paint!"

As Tom looked 326 over, John Green emerged from the chart room.

"Hi, John. Everything OK?"

"Fine," he replied. "We've had a few new additions. We have had radar fitted, and it comes with an operator. They've also changed the Brownings – 50-calibres."

" Bloody hell! That's going to increase our firepower," said Tom.

"We should be able to sink a bloody battleship now."

"Let's hope we never have to try," Lieutenant Green said.

"Come on – let's go and have a look at our orders," said Charlie. "We'll see if there's anything on."

Natalie was sitting at her desk.

"Anything on?" he asked her.

"Come over and have a look."

He picked up a sheet of paper. "What the hell's this?" he cried. "You are down for posting."

"Oh, that!" she replied. "Don't worry about it. It's only a short course – two weeks."

"Thank God for that! What's it for?"

"It's for my promotion," she said.

Tom said, "You'd better watch out, mate – you will be saluting her next."

"Oh no," he said. "We have an agreement: no saluting. We'll just make love more often."

"That's OK, then. You won't have time to do any saluting."

"Cheeky! Are you implying we are sex mad?"

"Well, no more than Caroline and I are!" Tom replied with a smile.

They all burst out laughing.

At that, the Commander walked in.

"Hello. What's all this hilarity about, then?"

"Oh, nothing, sir – just a private joke."

"I see!" he said with a knowing smile as he entered his office.

Charlie said, "What was that look for? Do you think he knew what we were talking about?"

Natalie smiled. "Well, he does have two children. He must have got them somehow, and I don't think he believes the stork leaves them under the gooseberry bush."

They all laughed again.

The phone rang, and Natalie picked it up.

"Yes, sir. The Commander wants to see you," she said.

"Sit down," the Commander said, motioning to a couple of chairs as they came in. "Make yourselves comfortable."

He produced a bottle of whiskey and three glasses.

"What's this – a party or a briefing, sir?"

"A bit of both, lads," he said, pouring three glasses.

"Cheers, sir!"

After a good swig, the Commander said, "OK, I will give you the news now. This job is a bit different to most. You are going to have to see how it works out as you go along."

"Hmm, that sounds interesting," said Tom.

"You will find it's that all right. The thing is, there is no strict timetable so you will have to play it mostly by ear."

"By ear!" Charlie replied. "We usually finish up playing most things like that anyway."

The Commander continued: "None of this will be written down, so there will be no chance of a leak. First of all, it's two boats again. Your destination is the coast of Spain. You will be picking up some special passengers who are coming in from Madrid. As you know, the Spanish aren't very friendly towards us, so that's the reason it has to be kept under wraps."

"Brilliant!" exclaimed Charlie. "Now we have to take on two enemies."

"Spain isn't exactly an enemy – more an unfriendly neighbour."

"Who are these people," asked Tom.

"They are Italian businessmen who don't like Mussolini. They are extremely rich and they want out."

"Couldn't they just catch a train out?"

"No, they are under house arrest, but they have managed to get word out to our lot."

"Why two boats?" asked Charlie.

"Simply, there are a lot of them." He told them as much as he could and ended the briefing by saying, "I know it's a bit sketchy, but that's all I have been told."

An hour later Tom and Charlie sat facing both crews in a Nissen hut.

"You start," Tom said.

"Right," Charlie started, "this is a strange op. We have to take 324 and 326 across to the coast of Spain."

"I've never been to Spain," someone shouted. "We'd better take our buckets and spades."

"We may need something more lethal than that," came the reply.

Laughter rang round the hut.

"Quiet! We sail for Spain tomorrow night at 2100 hours to pick up some Italian businessmen who are coming from Madrid. I will hand over to Lieutenant Weston to fill you in on the rest."

"Thank you, Lieutenant Higson. There's nothing too surprising about picking up a group of Italian businessmen, I know, but we will also be transporting their families."

"Bleeding hell, sir! Are we cruise ships now?"

Tom continued: "That's not all of it. Apart from wives, daughters and sons, their aides and older members of their families will be with them."

"That was no joke about becoming cruise ships, then," came a shout from the rear.

"That will be enough," responded Tom. "Do you have any serious questions?"

"How many all together?" asked Lieutenant Green.

"Possibly eighteen; maybe more. We will have to wait and see."

"That's going to take some bloody organising, sir."

"It certainly is, but Italian partisans are dealing with that end of it. We just need to get them on board and get out."

"Yes," said Charlie, "but if we get into a scrap, it could be a bit dodgy."

"Very bloody dodgy!" one of the crew chipped in.

"Is there a timetable?" one of the officers asked.

"Ah, that's one of the tricky parts," answered Tom.

"Sounds as if it's all bleeding tricky to me," one of them said.

"The only part we can be sure of is the rendezvous."

After the briefing broke up, John said, "I will go and get all the charts and study them."

"OK," Tom answered, "that's your department. Let me know when you have had a good look at them. Right, mate, let's get the boats refuelled and stores and ammo loaded."

As they walked down to the boats, Charlie said, "I wonder how long we will have to wait."

"I don't know, but we will have to cover the boats, and, at the same time, we will have to make sure we can get out quick if we have to."

"Don't forget it's a neutral country; so if we get caught, we could end up being interned for the duration," he said.

"Bugger that for a lark!" Charlie exclaimed. "We don't want that."

Final orders came through later that day. The officers squeezed into the wardroom on 326, where the orders were opened.

"Here goes! We sail tomorrow at 2100 hours. We top up at the Isle of Wight, then make for a place called Gijón, which is about 400 kilometres from Madrid. We should be able to make it in about twelve to fourteen hours. What's the weather, John?"

"The reports are for light winds, seas quite reasonable. There's a slight mist thickening later. If we can make 20 to 25 knots, we should make it by 0900 hours in the morning."

Tom continued: "We will be met at 0700 hours by a Spanish trawler, which will guide us to the inlet and top us up with fuel.

Hopefully we should get some word about our people. By the look of it, the inlet has plenty of cover for us. If anything has gone wrong, they should be able to tell us. We will post lookouts when we get in, but the Spanish partisans will patrol the perimeter for us. If we are spotted, we will have to put up a fight. It won't be Jerries; it'll be Spanish troops. The main danger will be aircraft while we are making for cover. OK, that's it. Let's do it and take it as it comes. Let's have a good meal and some rest and then go."

The light was going as they slid out of the harbour, and a slight wind picked up. The land took on a grey hue and the sea looked like lead. They passed the light bell, opened the throttles and set course for Spain.

It was a moonlit night, quite calm, with a light south-westerly breeze; the coast was a faint outline off to port; 324 was making 18 knots; 326 was two boat-lengths astern.

Charlie said, "Keep her steady and your eye on that light. I'm going down to the chart room."

"Aye, sir."

In the chart room, Alan was looking at the charts.

"Everything OK?" asked Charlie.

"Fine," Alan replied. "According to this, the inlet should give us plenty of cover."

"Good," Charlie answered. "When we arrive, Tom and I are going ashore to have a look around."

"Is that wise, sir," asked Alan.

"It's not in the orders, but we have decided to make sure we can get out quickly, and we need to be certain no one can sneak up on us."

"Well, in that case, it sounds a good idea," said Alan.

"Anyway," replied Charlie, "I've never seen Spain."

Alan looked across at Charlie. "You'll have to try the local brew, sir."

"Don't be bloody sarcastic, you cheeky young sod! Don't forget I'm the boss here," said Charlie with a smirk on his face. "I'll bring you a bottle back."

"Who's being sarcastic now?" said Alan with a smile.

"I'd better get back to the bridge before I put you on a fizzer," Charlie replied.

They both laughed.

"It's a good job we both have a sense of humour," Alan replied. "See you later, sir."

With that, Charlie returned to the bridge.

"Bloody dark, ain't it?" he said to Neil, his coxswain.

"I don't mind this so much. It's better than being too light. This way we can't be spotted as easily. Jerry isn't all that far from here," Neil said, motioning towards France.

"You're right," replied Charlie. "They could be on us in no time."

On 324, Tom was talking to John Green.

"Charts OK?" he asked.

"They have every detail you could ask for. Whoever did them knows this place well!"

"Good," replied Tom.

"I wonder what our passengers will be like," said John.

"Italian!" replied Tom.

"I know that. I mean, will they be full of themselves or what? They say the Italians are usually very vocal."

"I should think they will be very subdued. After all, what they are doing is very dangerous. I'd like to know how the hell that many people are going to get away without being spotted," said Tom.

"They must have it well organised," replied John. "Besides, if they are as rich as they say, they can grease a few palms."

"That's their business," replied Tom. "All I hope is that they appreciate what we are doing for them."

They were making steady progress. Tom checked the time: 0500 hours, and it was getting lighter.

"Well," said Tom, "it will be a bit more dangerous now."

"It will that," said Dave: "aircraft!"

"Yes, but I think we'll have to look out for subs too," said Tom. "I'm glad they let us keep the radar. I'll take over, Dave; you go get yourself some breakfast, then nip around the boat."

"Yes, sir."

With that, Harry came on to the bridge.

"Morning, sir."

"Have a good kip?" asked Tom.

"I did. It's nice when the sea is smooth."

"I'll check the radar. We're going to have to keep a good lookout now."

"I've asked Dave to go round the boat when he's eaten; I want you here with me in case anything goes off."

"OK," said Harry, "but I have a good feeling we might just get away with it."

"I hope you're right," replied Tom. "We'll know in a couple of hours when we get the boats camouflaged."

"I'll see to that," replied Harry. "We've got all the nets handy so we can get at them quick."

"Excellent! I won't be happy until we are in there and covered up," replied Tom.

An hour later they sailed into the inlet. It was just wide enough for the boats to turn around in – much to the liking of Tom. Charlie followed him in. They moored up and started to camouflage the boats.

After an hour, Tom and Charlie surveyed the work.

"Looks good, mate," said Charlie.

"Yeah," replied Tom. "We need to get a watch rota sorted out, and then we can go and have a look see."

"OK," Charlie replied, "is about thirty minutes OK?"

"That'll do," said Tom.

Tom and Charlie left the boat. They walked along a rough track, well sheltered by trees and bushes.

"I'm sure someone is following us," Charlie said.

"I agree," answered Tom. "We'll split up around that bend and see if we can spot him."

As they went around the bend in the track they split up and took cover. Two men came in sight. They were looking around when Tom stepped out with his revolver in his hand.

"Who are you?" he asked.

"Ah, señor," replied one of the men, "you will be Lieutenant Weston."

At that, Charlie came out.

"Well, I never! He speaks bleedin' English."

"Señor," the man replied, "we are sent to meet you."

"How do we know you're on the level?" said Tom, still covering them with his pistol.

"Commodore Harris told us what you looked liked," said the first man.

"Bloody hell! How do you know him?" asked Tom.

"I'm Lieutenant Commander Ray Stones, RN. Sorry about the surprise," he said, producing his pay book and identification. "I'm with the naval attaché in Madrid."

"Bloody hell! Someone could have told us!" Tom said.

"They couldn't," replied Lieutenant Commander Stones: "it had to be kept quiet."

"OK," said Charlie, "but what do we do now."

"This is Capitán Ricco Rodriguez of the Spanish police," said Lieutenant Commander Stones, introducing the second man. "He is a Spanish partisan."

"We'd better get back to the boats," said Tom. "You can give us all the gen there."

When they arrived at the boat, Tom introduced Lieutenant Commander Stones and Capitán Rodriguez to his crew, and they retreated to the wardroom.

"Is this place safe?" asked Charlie.

"Completely," replied the Capitán. "It is well off the beaten track; the nearest inhabited place is the village four miles away."

"It sounds safe enough. What happens now?" asked Harry.

The Lieutenant Commander continued: "Your passengers are being brought here from Madrid. There are sixteen of them."

"How the hell are that many people going to get out of Spain without anyone noticing?" asked Tom.

Capitán Rodriguez explained: "Their guard is made up of partisans who will escort them to the station after their conference. They will board the train with them under the pretence of taking them to the French border. At a junction just before Burgos they will be transferred to fast cars, which will take them to a rendezvous just outside Santander. There they will board a fishing trawler, and they should arrive here about an hour and a half after that.

"Sounds easy to me, if all goes to plan," remarked the coxswain.

"We will have to be prepared for any eventuality so our men will stay with them until they arrive at the boat," said the Capitán. "You must remember, Spain will not allow foreign troops on their soil. If the Spanish police were to become involved, then the partisans would fight them. If they were to call in help from the Spanish Navy, our hope is that you would assist. You appear to have enough firepower."

"If it comes to that, we will do all we can to help," replied Tom.

"That is all we ask, señor, thank you," replied the Capitán.

"Just one question," said Neil: "Why wouldn't the Spanish Navy help?"

The Capitán smiled. "Our navy isn't up to much. There may be some who would help, but unfortunately the boats we have in Santander are being watched by Germans."

"Right," said Charlie, "when is all this going to happen?"

"In two days' time."

"Will we see you again before then?" asked Tom.

"No," replied Lieutenant Commander Stones. "We're off back to Madrid in the morning. You will receive a signal when the trawler is at sea. This will be when it is dark, so you can set sail under cover of night to meet the trawler."

"What time will that be?" asked John Green.

"They will leave dock at 0200 hours. You have radar, I believe?"

"Yes," Tom replied.

"Our lights will be red over green on the bow, and the signal will they flash will be *Olé*."

"Oh, very Spanish!" said Harry.

They all laughed.

"Will you take a drink before you leave?" asked Tom.

"Thank you. Just a small one and then we must leave," replied Lieutenant Commander Stones.

On the day of the arrival of the passengers, Tom and Charlie were in 326's wardroom with John Green, Harry and Alan.

"We'll put to sea at 0100 hours," said Tom. "Do you agree, Charlie?"

"That should be OK," replied Charlie. "We can drift until we see them. What time do you expect to receive their signal?"

"ETA is 0400 hours, so that should give us plenty of time."

"We'll uncover the boats as soon as it gets dark."

"Agreed!" Tom replied.

"Fine by us," the others said.

"Waiting around all this time gives me the willies," Charlie said.

"Me too," replied Tom.

"It would be nice to have a good old-fashioned straightforward job for a change!" exclaimed John Green.

"We will have to get you one," said Alan.

Sitting on the deck were Bob Crowe, Stan Grey, Todd Soames, Les Wright and Jimmy Townsend.

"Tell you what," Todd said: "I'm beginning to get nervous with all this waiting around."

"I think we all are," said Stan. "It's the worst part."

"I know when we get back to Blighty I'm going to get drunk, and I intend to stay like that for at least two days."

"You get drunk!" exclaimed Bob. "You could drink a brewery dry and still not get drunk."

"What are you trying to say?" said Stan.

"Oh, me? Nothing. It's just that you seem to have a bottomless gullet when it comes to ale – and, after all, they don't make beer like they did in the old days."

"The old days! You're not old enough to remember the old days," Les said.

"Oh, I forgot you were around when Nelson was alive, Les."

"Cheeky sod!" he retorted.

They all burst out laughing.

"Well, at least we can still laugh," said Stan.

The boats were uncovered and waiting for the signal; Tom and

Charlie were in the chart room with John Green and the radar operators.

"Any time now, I should think," said Tom.

At that, the signal came through.

Charlie shook hands all round and said, "Here we go."

They all returned to their boats and made out to sea. They cut the engines and drifted in.

"Keep a sharp lookout, lads," said Tom.

Around half an hour went by.

"I hope nothing has gone wrong," said Harry.

"I've got them on the radar." A shout came from the chart room.

"About five miles; we should rendezvous in about twenty minutes. I'm picking up a signal to starboard as well – about two miles astern."

"Be prepared," said Tom. He hailed Charlie with this information.

"OK," shouted Charlie, "I'll get off in case it's trouble."

"There it is! I see a red over green – can't see the other one, though."

"Charlie will be on that if it's there," shouted Tom. "We'll concentrate on the trawler."

They drew close and there was a shout: "I think we are being followed," the voice said.

"Come alongside," Tom replied. "Our other boat will deal with them."

Suddenly Tom heard shots.

"They must have found the buggers," the coxswain said. "Get the passengers aboard; we can transfer them to 324 later."

The transfer was completed and their new passengers were taken below. Then they moved to check if 324 required assistance. The coxswain opened the throttle and Tom could hear the Bofors firing.

"That'll be 324," he shouted.

At that, they spotted them.

"As soon as you can, open up," shouted Tom.

They opened up the forward cannon and, as they did so, were joined by the twin 50-calibres; the tracer was finding its target.

The boat was a gunboat, judging by the size of it. As it turned away, there was a sudden explosion.

"They must have been carrying some sort of depth charge, poor sods!" Bob Crowe said. "They didn't stand a chance."

"They wouldn't have known much about it," said Stan.

Charlie came alongside 326.

"You OK?" shouted Tom.

"Yes – we've got a couple of wounded, though."

"OK, let's get this lot transferred across and get home."

It took fifteen minutes to get the transfer completed.

"OK," said Tom to the Chief, "let's go."

Dave opened up the throttle and the boat shot forward, picking up speed.

"Get her to 30 knots and then ease off when you think we are far enough out. I'll go and see our passengers," Tom said.

There were eight people in the wardroom: a gentleman who appeared to be in his fifties, his wife, two young girls of about sixteen or seventeen, a young man of around twenty-five, two children, and a young woman of about twenty-four (the young man's wife). The older man stood up as Tom entered.

"We cannot thank you enough, young man," he said, extending his hand. "I am Alberto Rossini; this is my wife Ana, my daughters Catherina and Isabela, my son Pepe, his wife Rosalina, and their two children."

"We're very pleased to have you on board, sir," Tom replied. "I will arrange to have some refreshments and blankets brought to you. We are making good speed and should be back in England early tomorrow."

Signor Rossini's wife took Tom's hand and said, "You are a very good and brave man, captain. May God bless you."

Tom looked at her and smiled. "We are very pleased to be of assistance, Signora. Thank you. We will make you as comfortable as possible."

With that, he left the wardroom and returned to the bridge.

"Well, John, they seem a very nice family. It's nice to know that we are helping good people," said Tom.

"It's not all about killing, is it?" John replied.

"No, it's not," replied Tom. "Well, take us home, Dave."

"I'll do that, sir, as quick as the boat can go."

"Right," Tom replied, "I'll organise a brew."

"That's the best thing I have heard all night," replied Dave.

Later, with a mug of tea in one hand and the other on the wheel, Dave thought, 'It's not a bad life, really – better than working down a mine!' With that thought, he took them back to England.

CHAPTER XVIII

Winding Up

The passengers were taken off and transported to a bus to be taken to London. Tom and Charlie shook hands. Signor Rossini thanked them both for everything they had done and invited them to visit when they were settled. Lieutenant Commander Dolin saw them off. He then came over to Tom and Charlie.

"Another good job you've done!" he said.

"Thanks, sir. It was all down to good teamwork and two excellent crews."

"I know that," replied the Commander. "That's why I picked you all out. Thank you again!"

"Is Natalie back?" asked Charlie.

"No, not yet. Her course finishes on Tuesday, and she should be back by Thursday," replied the CO.

"Oh, good!" said Charlie. "Can I get her number?"

"I have it in my office; I will dig it out for you," replied the Commander.

"I'm off to ring Caroline. We'll see you later, sir," said Tom.

"Tom, you might as well take a few days' leave," said the Commander.

"Smashing! Thank you very much, sir," replied Tom. "I think I will see if Caroline can get us a room at the hotel."

And off he went to make his call.

He had to wait quite a while to get a line, but he finally made a connection.

"Hello, darling," he said.

"Tom, is that you? Oh, how lovely to hear your voice! Where have you been? I know – you can't tell me!"

"Sorry I couldn't call – it was all rather hush-hush."

"That doesn't matter. You're home now. When am I going to see you?"

"This weekend. Can you book us a room somewhere nice?"

"Of course I can, and when you get here I'm going to lock the door and throw away the key until I've had my wicked way with you!"

"Sounds good! I didn't have any plans for the weekend," Tom replied with a laugh.

"Good, then you'd better get your strength up."

"I don't need to to make love to you, my darling. There's nothing else that gives me greater pleasure."

"Oh, you say the sweetest things! What train are you catching?"

"Hopefully, the 10.35, so I should be in for 1.45. I'll grab a taxi at the station and meet you at the hotel."

"I look forward to it," replied Caroline. "See you there."

The operator interrupted: "Your time is up, sir," and the phone went dead.

"Damn!" muttered Tom. "Surely I had more time than that! I know there's a war on, but still!"

When Tom returned to his room, Charlie was there.

"Did you get through?"

"Yes, thanks. They never seem to give me enough time, though."

"I know, but don't forget there is a war on," said Charlie with a smile.

'I can always rely on Charlie to cheer me up,' thought Tom.

"At least you got through; I can't get a line until eight o'clock tonight. So, what are we going to do now, then?"

"Well, I'm going to have a bloody long soak in the bath, shave and then go get a decent meal. And I think I'll finish the night off with a bit of a booze-up."

"Sounds good to me! I'll join you as soon as I've spoken to Natalie," said Charlie.

At eight o'clock on the dot, Charlie finally got through to Natalie.

"Oh, darling, I've missed you! I've been thinking of you all the time. I can't wait to see you."

"I've missed you too. How's your course been?"

"Oh, OK. The officer in charge said I shouldn't have any problem passing it. Hopefully, that means I should get my promotion as soon as there's a vacancy, but I don't want it if it means moving away."

"Oh, Nat, I love you so much, but I don't want to get in the way of your promotion – you've worked so hard for it."

"I know, but I'd rather be with you. Anyway, how's Tom?"

"He's in fine fettle – at least, he is now he's spoken to Caroline. He asked her to book a room for them for next weekend."

"Have you got leave too?" asked Natalie.

"Yes, but I don't intend to go anywhere until you have got back; the CO said Tuesday."

"I think I should be able to get away on Monday."

"Great! Do you think you could get us a room as well?"

"Your time is up," interrupted the operator.

The phone went dead.

"I see what you mean," said Charlie when he got back to the table.

"Told you, mate. I think I might write to Winnie and complain." Tom laughed.

"I'm sure that will work!" Charlie replied with a smile.

"Anyway, what are you having?"

"Another bottle of this if they will let us!"

They had a fine meal, and then retired to the bar to finish off the evening. The waiter came over and asked them what they would like.

"Two large gins," replied Charlie, "and keep them coming, please."

He handed the waiter a pound note and said, "That's for you."

The waiter looked at it, rather shocked, and said, "Oh, thank you, sir. That's very kind of you. I might get the wife something nice with it."

"How long have you been married?" asked Tom.

"Thirty-five years, sir," he said with a broad smile, "and still in love."

"Good for you!" they both replied.

When they got back to their room it was after midnight. They fell across their beds and were fast asleep as soon as their heads hit their pillows. It had been a long six days, but what was in store for them now? More excitement, more danger – that was for sure, and they both knew it. They were young, fit and a bit devil-may-care, but deep down they both knew there would be a price to pay somewhere along the line. They were like so many other young men in the services.

When Tom arrived at the Strand Palace Hotel, Caroline was waiting. She rushed up to him and flung her arms around him, and they kissed passionately.

"Oh, Tom darling, I just love you so very much. I don't ever want to lose you."

"There's no chance of that," Tom said, returning her kisses. "Nothing in this world could take me away from you, and that includes old Adolf and the whole bloody Reich. Until I met you I didn't know what life and love really meant, but I do now."

Some officers walked past, and one of them said, "Some people get it all, don't they?"

"Some people deserve it. Did you see the ribbon on his tunic?"

"What ribbon?"

"It was a VC."

Tom and Caroline were still in a long embrace. Caroline said, "Tom, I know we won't let anything or anyone spoil our happiness."

"Not likely, my sweet!" he answered. "I don't think there are two people anywhere who are more in love. Charlie and Natalie may not be far behind, but I doubt if we could meet anyone else that comes near. If they exist, then good luck to them."

"Oh, Tom, you say the most adorable things. It makes my heart leap. I haven't ever felt like this before." She squeezed his hands and said, "Take me to bed, my sweet."

It was dark when they finally left each other's arms, and they were both exhausted.

Tom looked at Caroline and said, "I think I am in paradise!"

Caroline looked deep into his eyes and said, "Paradise can't be as perfect as this. Nothing could be." She snuggled up to him. "I don't ever want to leave you."

"And I don't ever want you to," replied Tom; "but my stomach is telling me it's hungry, and, as the Good Book says, man cannot live on love alone."

"Well, the Good Book is wrong," Caroline said with a smile. "Whoever said that could never have been in love." With that, Caroline leapt out of bed. "Come on, then!"

Tom watched her as she walked across the room.

"I don't think I have ever seen anything so lovely," he said.

"Oh, I bet you say that to all the girls," Caroline said.

With that, Tom jumped out of bed and tackled her to the floor, rolling her across his knee as he did so. He smacked her bottom playfully.

"That's for being so cheeky," he said.

"Oh, do it again! I like it."

Charlie and Natalie joined them later that evening. They took in a couple of shows and they wined and dined. The time flew by, and all too soon they had to return to base.

Tom took Caroline to one side and said, "Sweetheart, sit down; I have something to tell you."

"You are going away, aren't you?" she said.

"Nothing is definite, but there is a possibility that the flotilla will be posted to the Med."

"Oh, Tom darling, we both knew that it could happen! I hoped and prayed it wouldn't, but I'm going to be strong for you because I know you are going to come back to me – Charlie too. Natalie hinted at it, and she said she would go too, so at least I know that there will be someone there to look after you both.

"Caroline darling, you are the bravest, loveliest girl I have ever known! I know we can win medals, and people say we are brave, but what you have to do when things like this happen goes beyond anything we can ever do. In my opinion, it's people like you who should get the medals. I'm going to do something, and you can't say no. I'm going to give you my Victoria Cross because I think you are far more worthy of it than I am."

"Oh, Tom, I won't say no. That is the kindest, bravest thing I think anyone could do. I will cherish and love it, and when you come home I will pin it back on your chest."

He took her in his arms; he didn't have to say a word.

CHAPTER XIX

The Move to the Med

Orders came through three weeks later, confirming that the flotilla was to be posted to the Mediterranean Sea. All the boats were to be sailed to embark from Southampton on transport ships. Each crew would take its own boat to be loaded by 23 September, and they would sail in convoy to Gibraltar. They would then be unloaded, and the flotilla would sail to Malta, where they would be based. An advance party, consisting of commanding officer Lieutenant Commander Dolin, Lieutenant Stephen Murray, Marion Baines and two Wrens from the ops room, Petty Officer Jim Welsh of Communications, Natalie James and four other technicians, was to fly out and prepare the base in Malta to receive the flotilla.

Tom managed a quick weekend away with Caroline. She told him that her decree absolute would be through by the end of October. Tom took her to a jeweller's shop and bought her the best engagement ring they could find.

"This means I will never ever leave you."

He also gave her his Victoria Cross.

They spent one more night together before he had to return to base.

"Tom, I won't come to see you off. You do know why, don't you? I will pray for your safe return every night."

"I promise I will come back to you, my love."

They had one last embrace and she watched him get on the train.

"Please, God, let him come back to me safely," she said to herself as the train left the station.

Two days later they left the base in Harwich for the last time, to sail to Southampton. On arrival, all the boats were loaded on to three transport ships with all their personnel. They were to sail in a convoy of twelve ships, with an escort of destroyers and corvettes, and a Royal Fleet Auxiliary aircraft carrier to provide air cover. It was to be a fast convoy with an estimated speed of at least 20 knots.

As they boarded, Charlie remarked to Tom, "Well, this is something we haven't done before."

The support crew for the new base were on board an ex-Cunard liner in the convoy.

"I hope Nat is OK," said Charlie.

"With all this protection we should all be OK. I expect Nat will be travelling in a little more comfort than we are."

In their cabin there were Tom, Charlie and John Green.

"It's sure going to be cosy," said John.

"You can say that again," replied Charlie. "Anyway, how's Phyllis?"

"Oh, she is fabulous – but boy, am I going to miss her!"

"I know what you mean," said Tom. "I'm going to miss Caroline terribly."

Tom then told Charlie and John that he and Caroline had got engaged and that he had left his Victoria Cross with her.

"God, I wish I had thought of something like that," Charlie blurted out. "Then again, I've not got your finesse, mate. That was a hell of a thing to do."

The convoy took four days to get to Gibraltar. On the journey there were sporadic attacks by U-boats, but they were beaten off. The corvettes sunk one and damaged another – a first-class job.

"Those boys certainly know their jobs," said John. "They're good boys. There's not a lot of comfort in one of those things, so I've been told."

"No, they were built especially as hunter-killers," replied Tom, "and they do a first-class job of it. Anyway, we haven't been too uncomfortable and the weather hasn't been too bad. What a difference in the temperature!"

"I wonder if it will be this warm all the time," said John.
"I wonder what they have in store for us," said Charlie.
"I'm sure we'll find out soon," said Tom.